LYNTON AND THE HAUNTING
OF
THE HMS WIND DANCER

By

J. Wayne Frye

Old Tale – New Twist

#14 in The Lynton Series

Lynton & the Haunting
Of the HMS Wind Dancer

TO:

Donald Chriscoe – In my youth, Carl Chriscoe taught me the art of salesmanship in a magical place called Jones Department Store, and, in the process, I met his son Donald. Donald and I forged a grand friendship for only one year, but it is a friendship I have always treasured, as we shared the exuberance of youth when the impossible seemed the probable.

Also, as always, to my muse:
Lynton Globa Viñas – the dynamic dynamo.

Catalogue Number: 971390-2019

ISBN: 978-1-928183-39-6

Fireside Books – Canadian Division
Part of the Peninsula Publishing Consortium

J. Wayne Frye

**Lynton & the Haunting
Of the HMS Wind Dancer**

Table of Contents

Lynton & the Haunting
Of the HMS Wind Dancer

<u>About the Author</u>

Wayne Frye's *Aaron Adams* mysteries, *Chablis Louise Chavez* thrillers, *Girl* books and *Lynton* adventures titillate the brains of those who enjoy tantalizing tales of mystery. Growing up in the small town of Asheboro, North Carolina, he wrote his first novel at 15, but waited over twenty years before finally submitting it to a publisher. His life, like the heroes he writes about, has been filled with adventure and excitement. He has been a college hockey coach, professor, and at one time, the youngest university president in the USA. Called a marketing genius by the *Los Angeles Times*, he has been a promotional consultant to hockey teams and motion picture companies. He has been cited for his work with inner-city gangs in Los Angeles. A proud Canadian, he divides his time between Ladysmith, British Columbia and Cape Town, South Africa.

<u>Some of the 46 books by J. Wayne Frye</u>

Hockey Mania and the Mystery of Nancy Running Elk
Something Evil in the Darkness at Hopkins House
White Meteors and the Ghost of Sue Ann McGee
How Hockey Saved a Jew From the Holocaust
The Girl Who Said Goodbye for the Last Time
The Girl Who Motivated Murder Most Foul
The Girl Who Stirred up the Whirlwind
The Girl Who Rode into a Storm
Fall From Apocalypse
Armageddon Now
Sammy Sasquatch and the Sts'ailes Star
Worth Part 1: Roaring Through Life Like a Comet in the Midnight Sky
Worth Part 2: The Night of Thunder Road
When Jesus Came to Jersey as the Son of Thunder
When Jesus Came to Canada to Lead an Indigenous Rebellion
When Jesus Came to the Black Hills to do the Ghost Dance
Lynton Curls Her Hair
Lynton Walks on Water
Lynton and the Vampire at Tagaytay Manor
Lynton Buys a Cell-Phone and Hears the Voice of Doom
Lynton Viñas and Beowulf Perez in the Taal Inferno
Lynton and the Ghosts in the Mansion on Balete Drive
Lynton Viñas: Shadow in the Darkness
Lynton's South African Adventure
Lynton, the Karoo Vampire and the Jewels of Omar Bin Abi
Lynton and the Stellenbosch Terror
Lynton and the Cape Town Ghost
Chablis: Avenging Angel for the Forgotten
Chablis and the Terrorist
Pursuit
The Disappearance
Points of Rebellion: Aboriginals Who Fought for Justice
Trumped in America

J. Wayne Frye

Lynton & the Haunting
Of the HMS Wind Dancer

Prologue
Taking Her to a Tomb

A mighty ship she was, but of evil born.
Oh, how she beckoned under the eerie moonbeam.
With the name Wind Dancer she'd been shorn
To be the transporter of an evil dream.

To those readers familiar with the famous dynamic dynamo, Lynton Viñas, it would be no surprise whatsoever that once again she found herself on the high seas seeking a respite from demon hunting and detective work that had so often brought her fame and glory, but had also raised the mild ire of her husband, Wayne, who insisted she not cause him worry as a result of getting involved in adventures that often put her in harm's way.

Affectionately calling her his little headache, he had sent her a ticket on the *HMS Wind Dancer*. She had a four week break in her doctoral programme, and he wanted her to enjoy a leisurely journey to Lagos, Nigeria where she was going to join him on his book promotion tour in a country where his books had become an overnight rage among adolescents. However, as she sat on the ship deck, she reflected back on the incredibly strange feeling she got when she first saw the ship in Cape Town Harbour.

The night before, as she approached the gangplank in the darkness, ticket in hand, one lonesome looking ghost-like totally expressionless deckhand stood at the top of the walkway. He was so thin that he appeared to be swaying as the notorious Cape Town wind howled. Moonlight poured from the sky like the milk of evil that was the sustenance of strange creatures that were waiting on a ship which was bound for stormy waters that would try men's souls and sow turmoil that would rage with a determined fury.

Although the far too often persistent Cape Town wind was howling and blowing, there was still an eerie quietness, the kind of extremely intense quietness one can sense in a graveyard at night. The people on deck stood or sat in stoic discontent like tombstones in that aforementioned graveyard. They were like giant monoliths rising from the solemn deck. Each one was picture perfect in form, polished and exactly the same as all of the others, except each one appeared to bear a different engraving on their stone faces. They were lined up perfectly with those in front of them and behind them, as if representing a processional of the dead in outdated clothing.

          J. Wayne Frye

Lynton & the Haunting
Of the HMS Wind Dancer

How could a place be so full and so empty looking at the same time? The people were not conversing with one another, only staring with blank dead-looking eyes at the dock below where no one was waving goodbye to them. Then again, how could human tombstones, with their faded etchings of distress, be more than a roll-call of people who cannot answer? For these people looked still and cold like cadavers.

Lynton walked aimlessly up the gangplank in the moonlight of an early warning that she unfortunately elected to not heed. She felt trepidation, but as always, she plunged ever forward unafraid with a willpower that bordered on the fanatical.

Owls fluttered by overhead, their silhouettes passing ominously over the ship, shadows seeming to dance about, embracing the darkness. Lynton took a deep breath and contemplatively thought to herself, "There are always many ships sailing to a variety of ports, but not a single one goes where life is not a challenge." In a world where incredible evil sternly predominated over good, she felt that maybe she should quickly turn around and flee with haste from the eerie feeling she was experiencing. Her instincts were always keen, and as she started to walk back down the gangplank, about mid-turn she noticed out of the corner of her right eye the rail-thin man beckoning her, motioning with his right hand for her to come on board. Almost trance-like, she turned back around, but he was not beckoning now. Was she imagining it? It made no difference, she was committed. She walked up, handed him her ticket and he summoned a steward to take her to her cabin. She felt as if he was taking her to a tomb.

 J. Wayne Frye

Lynton & the Haunting
Of the HMS Wind Dancer

Chapter 1
Universal Darkness Buries All

From the wild Atlantic her history she tore,
Over bounding seas she galloped on a breeze,
But something strange in the belly she bore,
That would make any observer with terror freeze.

Again, for those readers who are not familiar with Lynton Viñas, let it suffice to say that she is not only a woman of exceptional beauty, but as chronicled by her biographer, Wayne Frye, also a woman of extraordinarily perceptive powers of observation honed with an ability to ferret out the mundane and decipher that which is hidden from the untrained eye and mind.

As she sat on deck in the dead of the dark wrapped in a woollen blanket supplied by the steward, she seemed oblivious to her surroundings, but her keen powers of observation were actually taking in the grand sweep of characters passing by. Her delicate, soft brown skin glistening in the moonlight that was dancing across the deck paving it with shimmering slits of alternating black and white mosaics was a sight that the late-night strollers could not resist as they glanced over at her. Lynton's soot-black lashes were delicately matted and extended like a flittering gangplank of sensual delight. Her dark eyes twinkling with fluttering fascination seemed a perfect compliment to the calm night. This was not just a beautiful woman. This was a goddess-like vision, a Michelangelo, a Rembrandt of beauty and desire. As always, she was un-phased by the attention, because she knew that outward beauty was a fleeting thing that had little lasting value. She understood that character contributes to beauty. It fortifies a woman as her youth fades. A mode of conduct, a standard of courage, discipline, fortitude and integrity can do a great deal to make a woman beautiful at any age. And, of course, self-confidence adds to the mystique of a woman, and Lynton never wavered in her belief that she could tackle any adversity with dedication and fortitude, which made a seemingly bright light of assurance, courage and certainty emanate from deep within her that glowed like a strong beacon of determination.

She did not immediately look up as a gentleman took a seat beside her and wrapped himself in a blanket. Always friendly and cordial, she turned to him and said, "Good evening." He did not look at her, or nod any recognition but continued to stare off into the darkness.

J. Wayne Frye

Lynton & the Haunting
Of the HMS Wind Dancer

She did not want to disturb his contemplative nature, so she, too, went back to staring out at the darkness. Still, she could not keep from glancing over at him out of the side of her eyes. She could hear no apparent pattern of breathing from him. The charcoal greyness of the night and the fluttering moonlight cast an eerie glow upon the stranger. His age was indiscernible, but one got the sense that, although probably middle-aged, he appeared worn with years of adversity. His hair was long, tangled and greasy, and hung down, and you could see his dark, sad, lonely eyes peering through a deeply sunken face more bone than flesh. He appeared almost black with despair as was the night. There were no shades of colour to this poor creature, as on his face, where his face showed, was an intense darkness, a darkness that made a body sick, a darkness to make a body's flesh crawl. His clothes made him seem out of place on the somewhat luxury-laden ship – just rags, that was all. He had one ankle resting on the other knee; the boot on that foot was partially busted out, and two of his toes stuck through, but they appeared to have little flesh. They seemed skeletal.

Lynton shivered, not with fear, but with a feeling that was overwhelming her, a feeling that there was something about this man that was almost pleading for recognition. He would not speak, but maybe he could not speak, she thought. She didn't want to stare but her eyes kept flicking to the man, so still, so decrepit. The strollers did not seem to notice him, only she did. Why? Surely he was more interesting to look at than she was?

There was a mild interference at the far end of the ship as a man slammed the door to the main passengers' lounge. She turned to look at him, and then when she turned back, there was an empty deck chair beside her. The man was gone in the blink of an eye, and he was nowhere in sight. How could he disappear so quickly?

As time went on, and Lynton made small talk with a few of the passengers, a pattern of curiosity among them was growing about strange sounds occurring in the hallways as they went back and forth to their cabins. The passengers spoke of the ship in whispered tones, almost as if afraid to say out loud what they were thinking. Still, they all treated the matter almost as a joke; all, that is, except a young deckhand, a man named Warren Walton. Walton, who instead of laughing at jests on the subject, seemed to take the whole matter very seriously. This was his tenth voyage on the vessel, and although he avoided comment, the look on his face displayed a deep concern.

This made Lynton rather curious. She began to wonder whether there was, after all, some truth underlying the vague stories she had heard about dark shadows. Always inquisitive, she took the first opportunity to ask Warren Walton whether he had any reasons for believing that there was anything to the yarns about the strange goings-on aboard ship, because his facial expressions indicated such concern.

　　　　J. Wayne Frye

Lynton & the Haunting
Of the HMS Wind Dancer

How could anyone resist queries from someone like Lynton, whose beauty was disarming enough, but whose humble nature and exuberance of spirit penetrated any barriers or sensibilities that might be erected? Like that ridiculous anti-immigrant wall the buffoon of banality, Donald Trump, had once proposed, Lynton knew that no barrier could keep a determined person from scaling the heights of knowledge in a world where ignorance was promoted as a method of abject control. She was determined to climb the wall of denial erected on the HMS Wind Dancer.

It was obvious that Warren Walton knew things he had been told to keep to himself. After all, he was but a slave to the machinations of corporate overlords who refused to allow independent thought. Those who think are a threat to control. As a result of probably being told by higher-ups to avoid any discussion of so-called ghosts, he was, at first, inclined to be a bit stand-offish; but, resistance to Lynton's charms is an exercise in futility. To her probing inquiry he presently came around, and told her that he did not know of any particular incident which could be called unusual in the sense which she meant. Yet, there were lots of little things which, if you put them together, made you think a bit. For instance, it always appeared that each voyage was accompanied by bad weather. There always seemed to be only intermittent calm winds and sunshine was a rarity. It was if a dark cloud constantly appeared to surround the ship. Then, other things happened;

equipment that he knew had been properly stowed away and locked up was sometimes found outside the cases on the decks. Then, he said something that surprised her. "There is always a feeling in the hallways that can give you the shutters, because you feel like somebody or some thing is watching you. The shadows are really unnerving at times."

"Shadows!" Lynton said. "What do you mean?"

He lost the power of speech it seemed. He took a deep breath and let out a long sigh. He shook his head from side to side, appearing to silently say, "I am through talking." It was as if some unseen force had placed a clamp on his lips as they closed tightly, almost quivering from the force to keep his mouth shut.

Lynton looked at his blank stare and believed the truth of the matter was that he was, in a way, ashamed of having let himself go like he had in speaking out his thoughts about things he was not supposed to reveal. She surmised that he was the type of man with deep thoughts, but that he had been warned by those to whom he depended on for pay to not put any of his thoughts into words. Lynton saw it was no use asking any further questions; so she let the matter drop there. His silence was not abated. He turned and walked forlornly down the corridor. As he turned to his right at the end of the corridor, she noticed a shadow seem to be forming behind him as he disappeared around the corner. She scurried down the hallway, looking for Walton, but he had, along with the shadow, disappeared.

          J. Wayne Frye

Lynton & the Haunting
Of the HMS Wind Dancer

Although Lynton's natural proclivities toward adventure was piqued, the rest of the day was uneventful, and she told herself to do as her husband always said, "Stay out of trouble." After all, she was on a ten day cruise and was supposed to enjoy her break from the rigorous academic programme she had started two and one half years ago. She was within a few months of graduation, and would then make her final sojourn to Canada, where she would begin her new life in a new country with the man she loved dearly.

As the hours passed on the second day out, most of the few passengers she saw did not relate well to her gregarious, out-going nature, but she gathered a pretty general opinion growing among them that it was utter silliness about the ship being haunted. And then, just when Lynton was settling down in a comfortably relaxed manner, something happened that altered the sense of calm.

It was around 8:00 PM, and Lynton was sitting on the steps down to the promenade deck on the starboard side. The night was mild and there was a splendid moon peering through thick clouds above. To her far left, she heard one of the deck stewards, a man named Johnson, apparently quietly talking to a person unseen who must have been standing behind a column at the bow of the ship. Johnson sensed Lynton was looking at him, so he made a gesture to whomever he was talking with and stared over at her.

He waved at Lynton and walked toward her. He blurted out, "Unusual night ain't it, ma'am?"

"It is, yes," she said. But for some reason, she could not help but continue, "Almost a night so unusual that one expects a ghost to manifest itself on-deck."

"This here talk of ghosts is a lot of hooey. Just a pack of nonsense."

Just as the word "nonsense" was uttered, Lynton looked over his left shoulder toward the column where someone had apparently been standing while conversing with Johnson. Her gaze focused on a shadowy form of a man stepping from behind the column and moving toward the railing. Lynton stood up startled and did not speak as two passengers passed to her right and entered the main lounge. She glanced at them and then looked back toward where the figure had appeared. The shadowy manifestation was gone.

Observing the startled look on her face, Johnson said, "What is it?"

"Nothing," she replied, as she saw no need to alert him to something that was no longer there. Johnson nodded his head and walked away.

For a minute perhaps, she stood there, watching that area where she had seen the shadowy figure, but could see absolutely nothing. Then she walked slowly toward that column. From there, she looked around the corner and could see most of the main deck; where a few people were leaning on rails, looking into the vast darkness.

One of the older stewards, who had just delivered drinks to a newlywed couple on the deck to Lynton's left was meandering slowly back toward the double doors that opened into the lounge. And then, all at once, as she stood peering at those doors, she saw them slowly open as if some invisible hand had pushed them gently outward. There was no one there, only a dark shadow that floated outward as the steward went in without any acknowledgement that something strange was occurring.

The realization soon hit Lynton with intensity that she was either imaging things or that there were really dark shadows all about the ship, meandering about casually among the crew and guests. Was she hallucinating?

She realized that for her own peace of mind, she must settle, once and for all, whether the things she had seen were truly phantoms or the result of an overactive imagination. Her reasoning said it was nothing more than imagination, a rapid dream as she might have dozed off while standing or sitting without realizing it was caused by her extreme tiredness from exams and/or her recent adventure with a ghost in what her husband had chronicled in a book called *Lynton and the Cape Town Ghost*.

She observed the last shadow that came through the doors move down the deck-way, where it was joined by two other shadows. They had no real form, just a mist-like darkness that seemed to float about.

Determination overwhelmed her and she went straight for the shadows at a rapid pace. Suddenly, they rose into the air and seemed to fly forward down the deck. She walked over to the stern area, and looked in every nook and cranny, but there was nothing. Then she went under the stairs to the upper deck. It was darker under there than on the main deck. She looked all about, but the assurance nothing was there was not comforting.

She leaned her back up against the bulkhead, and thought the whole matter over rapidly, while keeping a glance about the deck. She concluded all she had observed was the result of an overtired and overactive mind. Then something occurred to her, and she whispered, "unless" and she went over to the starboard bulwarks and looked over and down into the sea; but there was nothing but sea; and so she turned and made her way forward. She was calm now and felt that her common sense had triumphed, and she was convinced that her imagination had been playing tricks with her.

She reached the double doors to the lounge, and was about to enter, when something made her look behind. As she did so, far down the deck to her left a dim, shadowy form stood in the wake of a swaying belt of moonlight that swept fluttering across the deck. It was the same figure that she had seen move from behind the column to the railing. She was not startled but did feel the hairs rising on the back of her neck. She was convinced now that it was no mere imaginary thing. It was a human-like figure. And yet, with the flicker of the moonlight and the shadows chasing over it, she was unable to see any more than a faint shape. Then, as she stood there just staring, she felt that

 J. Wayne Frye

her common sense assured her she was absolutely not hallucinating. Thus, she was determined to confront the thing, the apparition, the shadow, the dark spectre, whatever it was.

She moved toward it on the now deserted deck with determination borne from years of confronting the supernatural. She had gone half the distance, and still the figure remained there, motionless and silent in the moonlight as the roll of the ship became more intense. She was now confronting with a queer mixture of doubt and belief the reality that this was no figment of the imagination. She was drawing nearer. She was not ten paces distant when she felt an intense cold like when a person opens a freezer door in a hot room; when, abruptly, the silent, now undulating figure made three quick strides to the port rail, and dashed over it into the sea.

She rushed to the side, and stared over; but nothing met her gaze, except the shadow of the ship, sweeping over the moonlit sea. She stared down with disbelief into the water. For a moment, she was deprived the power of coherent thought. She was dazed and mentally stunned into a near comatose state.

*In vain arrives the all-composing hour
As the muse is called by the power.
She comes! She comes! The sable throne behold
Of night primeval and of chaos old.
Before her, fancy gilded clouds decay,
And all the varying silhouettes die away.*

Lynton & the Haunting
Of the HMS Wind Dancer

What shoots in vain its momentary fires;
The meteor drops, and in a flash expires.
As one by one, the dead strain,
The sickening stars fade off the ethereal plain.
Thus at Lynton's approach and secret might,
Shadow after shadow goes out and all is night.

She, seeking truth will not be fled,
As visions of dead ones pop into her head.
All this woman believed before
Shrinks to her cause and is no more.
Psychic of the metaphysic begs defence,
As she struggles of this to make sense!

Mystery and wonderment do fly,
As she gazes at those who long ago did die.
Religion blushing veils her sacred fire,
While those dead refuse to expire.
There is nothing in them to shine.
Gone is all that might be divine!

The dread of the dead is in store,
And one day this tale will become lore.
Light dies before the shocked eye,
As all life death cannot defy.
An unseen hand lets the curtain fall;
And universal darkness buries all.

     J. Wayne Frye

Chapter 2
Go Dynamic Dynamo, Go

*Aboard this doomed ship was not just the living,
As the dead there did make a frightening home,
And the dark shadows all about were unforgiving,
As they roamed under the black clouded dome.*

The next morning Lynton reflected on that apparition by the column and deduced that it was just one of many she had seen. She had another look at the places where that strange thing had been, and then reflected on how it left the ship to plunge into the dark sea below. She found nothing unusual, and no clue to help her understand the mystery of the strange shadows. She prowled about the decks, trying to discover anything fresh that might tend to throw some light on the matter. She was careful to say nothing to anyone about the strange occurrence. At this point, she noticed that the few conversive passengers seemed to have not experienced anything unusual.

Lynton & the Haunting
Of the HMS Wind Dancer

A woman was walking about the deck and stopped near Lynton. They stood by the railing looking up at the grey clouds that seemed to actually be following the ship, or more appropriately, moving with the ship as the skies were clear except for the ones hanging precariously overhead, seeming ready to unleash a deluge of rain upon the vessel. One of the vessel's mates, Harold Pinter, as most men do, was, as he stood nearby talking to a passenger, unable to keep his eyes off Lynton. Looking over the passenger's shoulder at her, the gleam in his eyes led to the assumption he was indicating an intense fascination with the dynamic dynamo.

Lynton was used to the stares of men, so she was usually totally unphased, but this man did attract her attention, because she realized he was doing more than just staring. He was moving his head upward as if while staring at her, he was also observing the clouds that seemed to be moving with the ship. He was sensing something ominous, and she knew it.

The woman by the rail walked away and as Lynton stood there, Harold Pinter continued to stare. She looked behind her back toward the column where she had seen the shadow. There, in the daylight, stood the infernal thing again. However, it was still too dark from the cloud cover to allow for any true discernment. Obviously, it was a man, but it was still more shadow than physical being. A person dies while the world, at once its mother and monument,

        J. Wayne Frye

remains. The person's name is lost, but the breath that was breathed still stirs the rustling leaves on trees, the sound of words once spoken echo on through space and time; the thoughts of the brain still float on the undulating seas under nights where the moon casts an eerie glow of discontent, passions never realized hang on the thread of spectres dancing in the darkness, the joys and sorrows that were once familiar friends wilt under the heat of lost opportunity now gone forever, the end from which all have fled wraps the arms of death around lost hope. Truly the universe is full of ghosts, not sheeted graveyard spectres, but the inextinguishable elements of individual life, which having once been, can never disappear, though ghosts do blend and change and change again forever. This thing Lynton saw she knew had died, but it still walked among the living. It was the un-dead dead!

There, standing by the railing, it seemed to her that she heard a very slight whisper. It was someone calling her name. She could not be certain, and at first she glanced forward to Pinter, who was still staring at her over another passenger's shoulder. She looked back and the shadow was not there, but she still heard the whisper of her name. There was no doubt about it this time, but she could not discern from where it was coming. There, suddenly before her, was Harold Pinter, who had left the passenger. He reached out his right hand and touched her left arm. She was about to ask him what he wanted, when he held up his finger to his lips, indicating silence should be maintained, and pointed forward toward the stairs leading to the deck above. In the dim light, his face showed palely, and he seemed highly agitated. For a few seconds, she stared in the direction he indicated, but could see nothing.

"What is it?" she whispered. "I don't see anything."

"Hush," he muttered in a low whisper, looking toward the stairs. Then, all at once, he was trembling, as he said, "You saw it too didn't you?"

"I am not sure what you mean?"

"The shadow in raggedy clothes," he said as he pointed to the stairs. "See right under the stairwell. It has moved there now, and I heard it, heard it whisper your name."

Lynton strained her eyes, but could not see what he was seeing, but then gradually she discerned a shadow of the man who had sat beside her under the stairwell, almost hidden, but, yes, she saw it.

He took her arm and led her toward the stairs. When they got there, the shadow had dissipated. Then, they looked back toward the stern and there by that infernal column was the shadow. How had it moved so quickly without detection?

Again, he grabbed her right arm as he looked at a lone figure heading their way and said, "It's the captain. Do not mention what we have seen."

At that instant, as the captain moved briskly toward them, behind him Lynton saw a crouching, slumped over shadow of a man, but so hazy and unreal that she could scarcely say she saw anything. Yet, like a flash, her thoughts ripped back to the figure by the stern column. She turned to look and then turned back. The figure was gone.

Deeper and deeper the shadow grew,
And about it was a determined evil.
The pulses of the clouds above
Began to move in a faster rhythm.
There was a twinkling cadence,
As the shadow floated about the deck.
It was still daylight but
Darkness permeated in silence,
And there was no contentment.
The whisper of a perished ghost
Settled like morning dew.
Across time the whisper came
From a voice long ago resolved
Into the primal silence to never twain.
A ghost, a ghost bringing evil and pain,
As in a spectral mirror wandering there.
Its pain outlived mortals to dare.

The captain stopped to exchange pleasantries. He indicated no knowledge of the strange occurrences on deck. Harold Pinter, winked at Lynton and excused himself, obviously indicating nothing about what happened should be shared with the captain.

Later, as night approached, Lynton sought out Pinter, whom she found in the lounge, staring out the window as he was having tea. There were many questions that worried her, and she, although told to stay out of trouble by her husband, could not help herself. This mystery of the shadows preyed upon her furtive mind that always sought out answers to what was often the unanswerable. She knew she should just let it go, ignore it all and not get involved, but how could she do that? It simply was not in her nature.

Pinter turned his head from the window, looked at her and seemed to beckon her with his eyes, almost pleading for her to take a seat across from him, which she did. His gaze was fixed upon her, and although nothing came forth from his mouth, there was an intense communication of fear in his eyes.

Lynton, her voice stern and direct, said, "Tell me what is bothering you."

"I have been warned to not discuss those infernal shadows darting about the ship with you. The captain knows who you are, knows your reputation. He knows you have detecting powers and have dealt with the supernatural many times. He wants nothing to cause any problems for the owners."

"And just who are the owners?"

"Who knows? A corporation that shields the rich from taxes and liability, no doubt."

Lynton, in a serious tone, said, "Welcome to the world of malfeasance and denial practiced by those who worship at the altar of greed."

"You are so right, there is but one concern of the captain and that is to see to it that he gets his bonus by making sure that the voyage is completed on schedule at maximum efficiency so the owners reap a tidy profit. Profit is all that matters to these people, and any strange occurrences must be ignored, because it might create rumours that could hurt the passenger business. The passengers are all gravy, because the ship also has a huge cargo hold, and therein lays the real profit."

"What have we really seen?" offered Lynton. "I mean dark shadows could be just the clouds and the moonlight playing visual tricks on our eyes and minds."

"You know that is not the case."

Sighing, Lynton replied, "Frankly, I have been in many situations where I doubted my own eyes."

"Do you doubt them when someone else sees the same thing as you?"

Lynton had no answer. She sat silent for awhile and said, "What do you think?"

"This ship is haunted."

"So," replied Lynton, "you have seen these dark shadows on other voyages?"

"Many times, but they have been getting worse, more frequent, more daring as time goes on."

"Have you talked about this with other crew members or passengers?"

"Yes, but the crew has been warned not to discuss this so-called foolishness with each other and to make sure we do not alarm the passengers by discussing it with them. We have been threatened with dismissal if we breech the orders in anyway, but frankly, I no longer care. I am tired of the whole sordid way this ship is run, anyway."

Lynton got up, looked down at him and pointedly said, "I never heed advice from those who want to avoid the reality of situations. The world has suffered great harm whenever good people have refused to face reality. I am not sure if what we saw was real or not, but I never discount any possibility. I am like a bloodhound in many ways, and I am on the scent of something sinister here. I can just feel it."

Lynton strolled out of the lounge, and as the door slammed behind her, she looked back and through the rounded door windows saw Pinter looking out at her. He had a look of deep concern. In fact, he appeared to be almost pleading with his eyes, pleading for her to somehow help him deal with what was obviously, for him, an untenable situation. She took a deep breath and headed toward the stern stairwell that led to her cabin. She did not see the strange shadow that seemed to be lurking in the darkness, following her.

She took out her key and inserted it in the door. As she did so, instinctively she looked back down the hallway. Nothing was there, but she felt a presence. She looked to the right where the stairs were hidden from view, and then she saw a long dark shadow casting an eerie glow on the floor. She shouted, "Who's there?"

The shadow scurried hurriedly back up the stairs. As it disappeared, Lynton decided to go up to the main deck in search of whatever it was. Breathing heavily, she turned and walked back down the hallway, then up the stairs to the main deck.

The night was exceedingly dark despite the light of the half moon; and the wind had dropped away almost to nothing, so that the ship was very quiet. Suddenly, she heard Pinter who came straight toward her as he shouted, "On the upper deck. Look!"

She walked gingerly toward him, but did not immediately look up. She observed him staring up at something that was hidden from her by a lifeboat. As she stopped and looked up, trying to see over the lifeboat, Pinter shouted again, "Look, look!"

Just then Lynton had moved to a position where she could see over the lifeboat. She saw what appeared to be a slightly built raggedly-dressed man standing to the back of the lifeboat. This was no shadow. This appeared to be the man who had sat beside her on deck just standing there, staring in the darkness toward the stern of the ship.

Who had gone aloft? Who would be fool enough to go there and just stand looking out into the darkness? Suddenly, a stern voice was heard to say to Pinter, "Go up there and find out who that fool is?" It was the voice of the captain who had come out on deck.

Pinter hurriedly ascended the stairs as Lynton stared in disbelief. Behind him was another crew member who had come on deck. The person by the life boat moved toward the stern and faded into the darkness.

"Well?" shouted the captain who was still on the main deck looking up.

"Nothing, sir," replied Pinter as he walked around the upper deck with the other crew member. They came back and went down onto the main deck with bewildered looks.

The captain said, "You saw nothing of him?"

"Nothing, sir," replied Pinter. "It was like he vanished into thin air."

The captain looked at Lynton, but had no words. She looked back at him and said, "Very mysterious."

He replied, "Nothing mysterious about some passenger going up to an area that is off limits. Happens sometimes. People can be fools."

"They can," offered Lynton, "and sometimes that which seems foolish can change when further examination offers a more profound explanation."

"I know you and your reputation," said the captain. "You need to mind your own business on this voyage. It would be best for all of us and especially you."

Lynton, very serious, with a look of intense determination, replied, "I hope that is not a threat, because I never take kindly to threats. In fact, I have been known to be even more defiant when they are issued."

Pinter, intimidated by the captain, but extremely impressed with Lynton's refusal to bow to his bullying, said, "She is a person renowned for her knowledge of the supernatural and for her investigative prowess, captain."

 J. Wayne Frye

"No mystery here," replied the captain, "just some fool causing trouble."

Just then on the upper deck, there was the man standing by the lifeboat again. Without an order, Pinter quickly scurried up to the top deck. Again, the man disappeared before Pinter got there.

"See anything?" shouted the captain as Lynton stood silently looking upward at Pinter.

"Na'!" said Pinter, tersely, as he walked toward the stern, obviously looking for the strange man. He had disappeared from sight.

Lynton, much to the displeasure of the captain, hurried up the stairs to the upper deck. She saw Pinter in the distance, and ran toward him. She was close at his heels, and he turned to look at her.

"What's up with you? The captain won't like you being up here."

"You really think I care?"

Smiling, he replied, "Definitely not."

He turned and said, "Come on, I am searching every nook and cranny of this deck."

As they scurried about the upper deck, the captain kept looking upward in silence. His expression indicated he was curious and concerned.

"Must be a blooming stowaway," screamed the captain up at the two.

Perhaps, thought Lynton for a moment, but then dismissed it. She remembered how that one thing she had observed stepped over the rail into the sea. That matter could not be easily explained and neither could this. She was, as always, curious and suspicious. She asked herself if they were merely chasing fancies of the imagination, or was there actually someone or some thing real among the shadows? Her thoughts kept returning to that thing that leaped over the railing.

Her train of thought was broken suddenly. Pinter, who had moved maybe 10 metres ahead of her was shouting and gesticulating. "I see him! I see him!" He was pointing upwards over their heads.

"Where?" exclaimed Lynton. "Where?"

She looked upward to the poop deck. She felt a certain sense of relief. "He is real then," she said. Still, she saw more shadow than man.

Down on the lower deck, the captain shouted, "Have you got him?"

"Not yet, sir," replied Pinter. "But I got him in sight."

Lynton realized she was seeing a shadow, not a real live man. She said, "I only see a shadow."

Just then, the shadow dissipated from view and Pinter said, "Gone."

"Then there's no one there?" asked Lynton.

"Na', guess not," replied Pinter

As they turned to head back down to the lower deck, coming toward them, with an expectant air, was the captain. "You've got him?" he asked, confidently.

"There wasn't anyone," said Lynton.

"What!" he roared. "You're hiding something!" he continued, angrily, and glancing from one to the other shouted, "Out with it. Who was it?"

"We are hiding nothing," Lynton replied earnestly. "There was no one up there. Nothing but a dark shadow, maybe caused by the clouds and the moon."

"You think I am a blooming fool?" he asked, rather contemptuously. "I saw him myself," he continued. "He was by that lifeboat. There's no mistake about it. It makes no sense for you to say he wasn't there."

Lynton took a deep breath and said, "Maybe he was. Maybe he wasn't. I am not so sure now just what I saw."

The captain said, "Pinter, you saw the man. I know you did."

"I think I did, but now captain I am not really sure."

"OK, so now neither of you is sure what you saw? Well, I saw a man I tell you. I saw a breathing, living human being by that boat. I say we have a stowaway on board – pure and simple."

"I don't think it was a stowaway, somehow," Lynton chimed in. "What would a stowaway want aloft? I guess he'd be trying more for a place below decks."

"You bet he would," offered Pinter.

Lynton began to postulate. "I have seen shadows in several places, unexplainable shadows. I am not discounting a stowaway, but I am just saying that there may be more than one anomaly here. There is something strange about this ship, something just not right, and captain, I believe you are hiding something, something that we should all know."

"Poppycock," the captain barked as he stormed off.

Lynton looked at Pinter and said, "Poppycock or not, I'm going to get to the bottom of this whole affair."

Smiling, Pinter in a near whisper, said, "Go dynamic dynamo, go.

Chapter 3
Life is a Daring Adventure or It's Nothing

*The HMS Wind Dancer by name
Was a ship that sailed in shame,
But on-board was one with a famous name
About to tackle spirits that from darkness came.*

It was on the next night that Pinter had the watch aloft, and he was still scanning all about for the mysterious man while Lynton was also prowling about with him as she had begun to treat the matter very seriously indeed. The taciturn captain had seemed to avoid her, but he did casually mention in one instance when he passed her that perhaps it was no stowaway after all, maybe just a roving passenger who feared being found in an area that was off limits at night. As Lynton glanced up at Pinter, their eyes locked on one another and she had very little doubt that he was beginning to realize there was something deeper and less understandable than he had at first shared with her. Yes, something strange was happening on this voyage, stranger than any of the other voyages he had experienced on the Wind Dancer. Still, all the same, she knew he had to keep his guesses and half-formed opinions pretty well to himself out of fear the captain would reprimand him.

Pinter had shared some knowledge with other crew members about the shadows he had seen, but they had been ragging him about being delusional and only wanting to see what would make him keener in the eyes of Lynton, whom they assumed had captivated him with her beauty and alluring ways. As he continued his watch aloft, they crept to the bottom of the stairs below where Pinter gazed out over the aft deck. He looked about and whispered to her, "I cannot understand how we have seen so many shadows, and particularly that dark figure that was by the lifeboat. Do you think all the shadows were that same person?"

"I am not sure," replied Lynton. "All I know is that there is something strange at play here, something that has apparently plagued this ship for many voyages, but the captain and the crew are reluctant to admit they have seen the strange occurrences. What is the reaction of others besides the captain?"

"No one wants to talk about it. Yet, the chief engineer grilled me about what I had seen, as it appears the captain did not share details, but he had heard of what happened. He shrugged it off as just fanciful foolery, but I could tell by his expression that he did not really believe that. He insisted I give him every detail I could remember about the figure we had seen by that lifeboat. What's more, the helmsman had not even affected to treat the matter lightly either, nor as a thing to be sneered at; but had listened seriously, and asked a great many questions of me. It is very evident to me that he was reaching out towards the only possible conclusion. Though, goodness knows, it was one that was impossible and improbable enough. He would not utter the word ghost, but I knew they both felt there was a mysterious presence or many presences on this ship, presences that had been here on many voyages, but that this voyage was different. This voyage seemed to bring about a more sinister intent. It was nothing concrete, just a feeling."

Lynton sighed and replied. "We have eight more days on this voyage, and I will not rest until I somehow find a plausible explanation, or even an implausible one."

"I am with you," offered Pinter, as Lynton bid him goodbye with a smile and an acknowledging wave of her right hand.

It was on the following night that another element of fear was manifested. And those who had seen nothing previously would find little to not be afraid of in a Nigerian flag that flew on the main deck. They were much puzzled and astonished, and perhaps, after all, a little awed. There was so much in the affair that was inexplicable, and yet again such a lot that was natural and somewhat tragically commonplace. For, when all was said and done, it was nothing more than the blowing adrift of a Nigerian registration flag banner that had been flying above the main deck. It appeared insignificant, but not so insignificant in light of what the captain, Pinter and Lynton knew.

It was around seven o'clock in the evening and few people were on deck. Suddenly, one of the stewards, as he came onto the port side deck from the cabins entryway, was nearly wrapped up by the banner that had apparently broken loose. There was a puzzled look as Lynton and Pinter glanced at one another while the banner blew off and fluttered all the way aft and stuck on the railing.

The captain shouted down from the top deck where he was doing his 7:00PM deck check at the steward and said, "Secure that banner, now."

"Aye, aye" shouted the steward.

He grabbed the banner and made his way forward, climbed up on a bench and started to reattach it. Lynton stood stoically observing him, as did Pinter. They could see him with a fair amount of distinctness, as the early half moon was slightly peeping through a small opening in the very dark clouds overhead.

Lynton went over to the weather pin-rail as Pinter stared down at her and leaned up against it, watching the steward. The other few people on the deck had gone aft, seemingly uninterested in what was happening, so that Lynton imagined she was the only one about the main deck. Yet, a minute

     J. Wayne Frye

later, she discovered that she was mistaken; for, as she glanced back over her shoulder, she saw the captain descend the stairs and step onto the main deck, turn and look up as the steward went steadily up the extension ladder to reattach the banner. The few passengers there had all departed.

There was something sinister looking about the captain thought Lynton. She stood and contemplated why he would be so interested in a banner that had broken lose. Obviously, the steward was making sure it was safely reattached, but the captain she realized was not looking at him after all. He was apparently in deep thought.

She remembered the unaccountable emphasis he had laid on that so-called stowaway; and reflecting on that, she felt a sudden sense of trepidation. For, all at once, the absurdity had struck her about the blowing adrift in such fine and calm weather of the banner. She wondered why she had not seen before that there was something queer and unlikely about the affair. Banners do not blow adrift in calm weather, with the sea tepid and the ship as steady as a rock. She moved away from the rail and went to talk with Pinter as he descended the stairs. He knew something, or, at least, he guessed at something that was very much blankness to her at that time. To their right, the steward was climbing up. That was the thing that made her feel concerned. Something simply was not right. There was a feeling; a pall of darkness had been their constant companion since leaving port. Ought she to tell all she sensed and guessed to Pinter? And then, just as she was about to unburden her feelings to him, he whispered, "It has started again. Will it never end?"

"What? She said.

"That banner."

She glanced up, looking directly into his eyes, as she said, "What is so strange about the banner blowing down?"

"It is not the banner. It is what happens after it blows down. Long ago, on the very first trip to Lagos, it blew down twice. Within a few hours, after the first time, one crew member was lost overboard and after the second time another was found in his bunk apparently comatose with fear. He was unable to speak. An ambulance was waiting on arrival. No one ever shared what the doctors said, but rumour is the man was put in a mental institution, as he, upon coming out of an apparent coma, kept shouting about the shadow coming for him."

"Was there not an investigation by the authorities?"

"Sure," replied Pinter, "but what can they do? There was no foul play from all indications. Besides, the authorities in Cape Town and Lagos are used to strange things happening on this ship. A passenger even disappeared once, and it was assumed, after the police investigated that he must have jumped or fallen overboard. Then, there was another time when a lounge singer claimed she was being followed by a dark shadow every time she went down the main hallway late at night. She

 J. Wayne Frye

even claimed it touched her once. She refused to walk to her cabin without an escort. She quit once the ship made port.”

“And the authorities did not investigate?”

“It was never reported.”

Sighing, Lynton offered the normal explanation for avoiding controversy in a world where greed prevailed, “Afraid of how it would affect the bottom line. Same old story.”

“Afraid so, yes.”

“And there is no need to query the captain any further, because, no doubt, he refuses to accept any explanation that might create rumours that would affect business. He will do all that is possible to hide this from public scrutiny.”

“You got that right, but despite telling us all not to gossip, word has gotten out, and it is getting more difficult to control the crew. We are actually being paid above the norm, apparently because of all the strange occurrences.”

Lynton stood irresolute, as she was positively stumped what to do. Her husband would say, “Put it aside. Don’t get involved.” Still, she knew she could not just shirk it off. That there was danger lurking about, she was convinced; though if she had been asked her reasons for supposing so, they would have been hard to pinpoint. It was more a feeling than anything concrete. Yet, her intuition always served her well. She was certain about the shadows as her eyes had already observed them. She had witnessed the supernatural often, and this particular time, from what she assumed, there simply was no definitive explanation for what she had seen.

She bid Pinter goodbye, and while she walked toward the stern, she glanced back over her right shoulder as the steward, attaching the last banner baton suddenly tumbled from the ladder, hitting the deck with a thud. She and Pinter both rushed toward him and the captain bounded down the stairs. The steward lay there staring up with glazed eyes toward a dark shadow on the upper deck. Lynton knew that stare. She had seen it far too often. His neck was obviously broken as his head dangled to the right of the deck. He was dead! The shadow flittered away in the darkness while the three of them stared in amazement. They looked intensely at one another.

The captain whispered to Pinter, "Quick, get some crew up here to take the poor soul below. Put him in one of the empty freezer lockers. Keep quiet about this." Then he looked over at Lynton as he continued, "And you'd do well to keep it quiet, too. No need to concern the passengers, as it will dampen their vacations. I am sorry you saw it. I'll arrange to refund your fare."

It was obvious to Lynton he was offering a bribe to keep her mouth shut. She replied, "I'll keep quiet for the very reason I see no need to alarm or to sadden the passengers with the burden of a death on the voyage, but I do not need to be bribed with a refund. I see something sinister going on here, and I will not be rest until I get to the bottom of things."

     J. Wayne Frye

Lynton & the Haunting
Of the HMS Wind Dancer

As Pinter left to get the crew members for removal of the body, the captain said, "You'd be well served to curb your inquisitive nature."

Just then, another steward walked over with an inquisitive look. Suddenly, the banner swept down again and wrapped itself around him, making him stumble blindly backward toward the railing. The banner completely engulfed him, seeming to actually lift him up. He was going to fall over the railing. Half his upper torso was already almost over it as the captain moved quickly toward the railing.

The steward was flailing away inside the banner. Pinter and the two crew members rushed toward the banner, grabbing it and frantically fighting, along with the captain, to prevent it from pulling the steward over the railing into the swirling sea below. As they struggled with it, Lynton stood apart intensely observing.

Finally, the four men managed to pull the steward back onto the deck and untangle him from the banner. The banner crumbled to the deck and then a gust of wind seemed to lift it up. It floated toward the upper deck, and it landed in a lifeboat where a dark shadow stood. All there were mystified and awed. The captain shouted, "Get that body below decks, now!"

As they scurried to obey, Lynton never took her eyes off that shadow. The captain, standing by her side, said, "What is it?"

Lynton replied, "That is what I am going to find out," as she leaped quickly up the stairs like a gazelle on the plains, moving toward the damnable shadow while the captain stood in surprise at her incredible swiftness.

She reached the top of the stairs, and moved quickly toward the lifeboat. The shadow was perhaps 10 metres from her. She was surprised when the captain appeared by her side and said, "Let's get that thing."

Then, as the captain moved toward the shadow with Lynton by his side, the banner rose up from below like magic and wrapped itself around him. The banner floated toward the deck railing and Lynton knew she had to act fast to save the captain. She ignored the shadow that was standing there in the boat with outstretched arms.

She moved quickly toward the banner that had encircled the captain. Strangely enough, even at that moment, the thought came to her how little wind there was. Yet, the banner, as if guided by that shadow, had flicked across the deck as if in a whirlwind.

Lynton grabbed the banner's rope ties and made a running bowline with them around the railing, as the captain's head peeked out. Then she tightened it again and again around the railing. A second later the captain had managed to untangle himself and stood exhausted, finally collapsing safely on the deck. In the uncertain moonlight peeping through the clouds, the two of them could just make out the shadow that was now floating at the far end of the deck. As they stood there a moment, still a bit discombobulated, they caught the sound

     J. Wayne Frye

of Pinter's voice close beneath them. They glanced down; then he looked up at them and gave a sigh of relief that they were all safe.

"Look," he said, as he pointed to where the shadow had floated. There it was, now undulating and bouncing about near the aft railing. They all stood in spellbinding awe.

Bounding up the stairs, Pinter arrived by their side and pointed again as the shadow seemed to fall backwards over the railing into the darkness.

To Lynton it seemed that there was as much bewilderment as anything else among the two men. The captain glanced up at her and seemed about to say something. Then, seeming to change his mind, he turned his head looking at the spot where the shadow had disappeared. Lynton broke the silence. "This is not going to end well, I fear."

The captain replied, "Missy, you need to butt out of this whole affair?"

"No captain, what you need to do is stop worrying about the bottom line for your corporate masters, and start worrying about the safety of your passengers."

Boiling with anger at Lynton's boldness in calling out his mercenary tendencies, he said, "I am the captain of this ship, and I am lord and master here. You would do well to remember that."

"Captain, I do not take kindly to threats. In my world, I accept no lords and no masters. I have a mind, and unlike the majority of people I do not bow subsequently before authority."

Lynton & the Haunting
Of the HMS Wind Dancer

When in the course of human events there are those who dare erect a barrier to truth, there is often found a paragon of virtue named Lynton Viñas, who like a mighty gladiator of righteousness stands as a bulwark in defence of justice for those who far too often receive none. She had witnessed the death of a man who would be sacrificed at the altar of greed by hiding the truth in order to keep the largesse rolling into the corporate coffers of the ship's owners. The captain was but a vassal in service to the greed which had made a mockery of justice all across the world. There was perhaps only one small island nation left where greed had been kept at bay, and for many decades it had suffered at the hands of the American government that wanted to force it into submission to the culture of greed like the rest of the world. Lynton had stood by that island nation's leaders years ago, when her husband took her to Cuba, where he introduced her to Fidel Castro, a man too strong to bow before the American nation that wanted to turn the world into America incorporated. She had also often heard her husband's orations about the true hero of the Cuban revolution, Che Guevara, and how he was targeted for elimination by the USA for daring to espouse for a world where the poor were treated equally to the rich. That was sacrilege which would not be tolerated by governments devoted to serving the interests of the few at the expense of the many. However, Lynton would never bow before the evil of exploitation and greed.

 J. Wayne Frye

Lynton & the Haunting
Of the HMS Wind Dancer

The captain, irate at what he considered impertinence, shouted indignantly at Lynton, "What do you mean not bowing to authority. I am the authority on this ship."

Lynton replied, "I don't mean any impertinence. I mean that I accept no authority over my right to think for myself."

"I tell you it won't wash!" he shouted. "No one should spread unfounded rumours."

"It's not about rumours. It is about something mysterious going on here," Lynton answered. "You ought to understand that. What we have seen is abnormal, and it needs clarification through a thorough investigation."

"What do you really mean?" the captain asked, quickly.

"Well, sir," Lynton said, "to be straight, what of the rumours I have heard from people about strange occurrences in regards to shadows and accidents in the past? Rumours are not always credible, but they do need to be investigated."

"That will do!" he said, angrily. "I won't entertain any talk about nonsense." Yet there was something about his tone that told her she had actually reached him, maybe penetrated a little of his intransient attitude. He seemed all at once much less able to appear confident that she was spinning a fairy tale. In fact, he knew what he had seen, and was now beginning to sense that this woman might well be beyond control, as she obviously had a determined will that would not be stayed by threats.

Lynton & the Haunting
Of the HMS Wind Dancer

After that exchange, for perhaps half a minute, he said nothing. Apparently, he was doing some hard thinking. When he spoke again it was with much less arrogance. Obviously his respect for Lynton was growing. He looked into her piercing dark eyes and said, "I saw something strange, but my guess is it was a passenger or a stowaway. It was nothing more, nothing as sinister as you are intonating."

"I intonate nothing, sir. I go by cold hard facts, but I, through years of experience, know there are some things that defy explanation. Still, I never stop searching for an explanation."

The captain chose his words carefully as he thoughtfully said, "That flag banner simply broke lose in the wind and that happens on occasion. Nothing mysterious about that really."

Lynton, just as thoughtfully said, "There was no wind, and it wrapped around you. What caused that to happen two times? You were lucky to survive."

"Must be a feasible explanation."

"And the shadows?" offered Lynton.

"Just a reflection caused by the clouds and the moon peeping though. That's all."

Smiling, Lynton replied, "Yeah, like you really believe that."

Pinter said, "I believe…" and then stopped.

"Go on!" said Lynton. "Spit it out despite your fear of the captain."

Looking over at the captain, he stuttered, I, I."

"Say it," shouted the captain.

 J. Wayne Frye

Still, he hesitated. "I am tired of all the fear, all the keeping quiet. The crew has had enough. I have had enough."

"Then speak your mind," said the captain.

"There was no wind either time and you know it, captain. And you know there was a shadow, a dark shadow on the upper deck. No matter how you try to explain it, the shadow was real, and I say it was no ordinary man."

The captain, his anger being held in check, said, "Look, I admit this ship has been plagued with strange occurrences, strange things that defy explanation." He then looked intensely into Lynton's eyes, and she wondered by his gaze if he was beginning to realize that it would be prudent to try and find a plausible explanation to what had happened. Had he begun at last to couple what had just occurred with the peculiar happenings previously?

After staring a few moments at Lynton in a doubtful sort of way, he very calmly said, "And what of you Miss Demon Hunter, I can see the wheels turning in your head. What diabolical plot do you think is unfolding on this ship?"

"There are times when one must simply face the fact that there are unknowns in this world that may never be known. This mystery of the shadows and strange occurrences on this ship could be in that category I am afraid, but I am not one given to accepting anything without a very thorough investigation and thoughtful analysis of all the facts."

Lynton & the Haunting
Of the HMS Wind Dancer

The captain sighed in exasperation, and as he walked away, he looked back over his left shoulder and said, "Go at it then dynamic dynamo, but tread very lightly, because I will not tolerate the passengers being inconvenienced or panicked by any wild tales or mishaps promulgated by your inquisitive nature."

Lynton looked at Pinter and said, "Did he just give me the green light to investigate?"

"He did, but my suggestion is to do exactly as he said about treading very lightly."

"There's an old song my husband sings about a mountain boy moonshiner and there are a few lines that go:

> *Roaring out of Harlan,*
> *Revving up his mill,*
> *He shot the gap at Cumberland*
> *And streamed by Maynardville.*
> *With G-men on his taillights*
> *And roadblocks up ahead,*
> *The mountain boy took roads*
> *That even angels feared to tread."*

Pinter looked at her and said, "And you are about to tell me that you are no angel and have no fear to tread anywhere, anytime."

"You got that right my friend. Avoiding danger is no safer in the long run than outright exposure. Life is a daring adventure or it's nothing."

     J. Wayne Frye

Chapter 4
Often, There Simply is no Explanation

*As thrilling ghostly sea legends go,
Did spirits on this ship dance in ecstasy,
After rising from their abominable lairs below
To embrace some evil dark apostasy?*

Lynton got into the ship's library to research the background of the ship. Its original name was Dark Lady and the vessel lived up to the name. It took a laborious effort utilizing a variety of books to finally arrive at what seemed a cogent rendering of the history of the ill-fated ship. Building it at the Cape Town shipyards in 1948 was a long and tedious process where strange occurrences plagued construction. Although it was a staunch and strong vessel, there was one disaster after another that made many men walk off the job, refusing to finish what they called a doomed ship.

Finally, with no one willing to work on it after three men were killed, falling from the deck to the concrete 60 feet below, and other men being maimed and injured in various mishaps, the vessel was dry-docked, sitting out in the elements for years until a company bought it for a mere one million Rand with the promise to refurbish it and make it into a passenger liner. In the process, another man was killed by a banner that had been hung up to promote the corporation. It simply, on what seemed a windless day, blew down from a temporary mast and wrapped around the man who was painting the deck, seeming to lift him up and over the safety railing, dragging him to his death on the concrete below the platform on which the ship had been dry-docked. The following week, a foreman was berating men for gossiping about the apparent doomed nature of the vessel, and as he stood on the promenade, a rigging rope on the upper deck broke lose at one end, wrapped itself around his neck and decapitated him with the precision of a guillotine.

Unable to find anyone to work on the vessel in Cape Town, the company sailed it to Dover, U.K., where it was finished. There were no mishaps in Dover, and the company registered the ship in the U.K. and renamed it the HMS Wind Dancer.

Lynton actually found a diary in some of the U.K. maritime archives aboard from 1955 that was compiled by a seaman named Howe. According to the diary, when the vessel left Dover to sail to Cape Town a man named Dartano was captain of the vessel. He threw his heart and soul into his work. He gave great grace to being a captain.

Lynton & the Haunting
Of the HMS Wind Dancer

Before leaving on the voyage to Cape Town, he had proclaimed the ship as goodly and strong. However, on the way there, he soon seemed to be overcome with a fearful soulfulness of spirit, and he would often be seen standing next to a large column at the bow of the ship. Men on the bridge would look out at him as he seemed, with animated hand gestures, to be conversing with someone behind a large column. The person with whom he was conversing could not be seen, but there often appeared to be a thin dark shadow visible in the moonlight.

Then, just a few kilometres outside Cape Town Harbour, the captain, as he was standing in his usual spot on the bow conversing with somebody behind the column, abruptly turned and held his hands out seeming to plead in great fear. He backed to the edge of the bow and fell over the high railing still seeming to plead at somebody or some thing hidden from view.

The first mate on the bridge ordered full stop, but the captain apparently sunk under the ship and was pulled into the propeller blades. His body was never recovered.

The diary by Seaman Howe had been preserved as evidence in the investigation, but the Cape Town Harbour Board of Inquiry simply concluded that the captain had accidently fallen overboard.

The archives were old and dusty, as she put them back. Lynton sat in her chair mulling over what had occurred on that faithful voyage. There was something sinister afoot then and now!

Lynton & the Haunting
Of the HMS Wind Dancer

The next morning Pinter walked up to her as she was strolling about the deck in deep thought and whispered, "Something happened last night."

Lynton, with concern, said, "I am almost afraid to ask what?"

A look of fright on his face, Pinter offered a harrowing tale. "The chief engineer was in the hallway on the main deck, heading to his bunk. He felt uneasiness as he walked down the hallway. He had the feeling that somebody was following him. Yet, he feared turning around. He stopped at the end of the hallway, and turned to his left to go toward the bunk room. As he did, he saw an undulating shadow at the other end of the hallway as the lights dimmed to almost total darkness. Then the lights began to flicker, and he saw the shadow swiftly moving toward him. He ran toward the bunk room, went in and slammed the door. He stood in bewilderment just waiting for that shadow to somehow come through the door. His heart palpating with fear, he could not move, but then, as he stared at the door, he felt there was something behind him. He looked down at the floor and in the pale light saw the reflection of a dark figure standing behind him. He did not turn to face it. Rather, he bolted toward the door, forgetting his fear of what was on the other side, and quickly pulled it open. There stood the dark shadow, again menacingly undulating. Trapped between the two shadows, he let out a scream. He heard absolutely nothing from the shadows. He bolted to the left of the hallway shadow and fled,

     J. Wayne Frye

never looking back and simply bounded up the stars.

"He ran to the bridge, where the captain greeted the whole tale with scepticism, asking him how much he had to drink. Without hesitation, the fellow simply said that the captain could make fun of him all he wanted, but that this would be his last voyage on this infernal ship."

"My friend," replied Lynton, "I am not one to live in fear, but I am afraid that this is more than just a casual haunting of an ill-fated ship. I believe there is something deeply diabolical going on here, something that is about to come to full fruition on this voyage, something that has been building for years, something that is deeply rooted in the history of this ship. I fear time is short, so short that we may all meet our doom if we do not get to the bottom of what is occurring."

The two of them found the engineer making his rounds, a man named Williams, and Lynton said to him in a no-nonsense, straight forward manner without even waiting for an introduction, "Did you attempt to touch those shadows?"

"No," replied Williams. "Do I look like a fool?"

"Absolutely not," offered Lynton. "However, I am curious if there is more there than just an undulating shadow. Our minds can play tricks on us when we are afraid. And there is no shame in being afraid. Being afraid is often what keeps you alive. The strange occurrences on this ship have apparently been going on for years. Now, I know that the reason it still plies the sea is greed, for that is, unfortunately, the prime mover of commerce the world over."

Pinter, a look of disdain on his face, offered a cogent observation. "The owners of this ship have always put profit before people. They have done that for years, which is why they do all they can to keep these strange occurrences, these deaths, these manifestations of evil quiet. Frankly, I get the feeling, for some reason, that this has all played out before. It is like I am living in a dream. Williams here is a well-schooled hand, and what he saw can be taken to the bank. When he says something, I believe him 100%."

"It's queer," said Williams, in a puzzled voice. "There doesn't seem to be any way to arrive at a proper explanation about what is going on."

Lynton glanced quizzically at Williams to suggest that he perhaps might know more than he was revealing. He, seeming to read her intent, shook his head, and, after a moment's thought, it appeared that there would be nothing more forthcoming. The three had no clear idea of exactly what had happened on the voyage and the half facts and guesses would only have tended to make the matter appear more grotesque and unlikely. The only thing to be done was to wait and watch. If they could only get hold of something tangible, then they might hope to tell all that they knew, without being made into laughing-stocks. But how were they to do that?

The three of them shrugged their shoulders and went about their business. Yet, everything had been laid bare between them in a subtle and tangible way, and, indeed, so was the affair, that only those who had actually come in touch with the invading fear seemed really capable of comprehending the terror of things, but even they were struck at how there was no discernable explanation for what they saw. For many, the explanation was simply that the ship was unlucky, and, of course, some attributed it to vivid imaginations titillated by strange tales.

Lynton thought that the captain was certainly concerned; though she did not think he was grasping the real significance that underlay the several queer matters that had disturbed so many and actually caused deaths. He seemed to fail, somehow, to understand the element of personal danger that, to Lynton, was already plain. He lacked sufficient imagination, she supposed, to piece things together, to trace the natural sequence of the events and their development. As it was, he had not seemed to reach out at all, but rather, attempted to cover up all the strange occurrences with implausible explanations. However, after seeing something first hand in the darkness of reality with Lynton by his side, he had begun to realize that this voyage might indeed be ill-fated.

The following night, it was a partially clear, star-lit, moonless sort of evening. The wind had picked up a bit; but still remained steady. They were slipping along at about 12 knots. It was the middle watch on deck, and the ship was full of the blow and hum of the wind aloft. Lynton had been invited to the bridge as a gesture of respect from the captain. Pinter stood by her side. The captain asked them if they would like to stroll the deck with him on his 12 midnight check about the ship. The late hour found them alone on the main deck. Suddenly, overhead, there sounded a sharp crack, like the report of a rifle shot. It was followed instantly by the rattle and rumbling of that infernal banner thrashing in the wind.

Pinter turned and ran aft a few steps. Lynton and the captain followed him, and, together, they all stared upwards to see the banner flying in the wind. Indistinctly, they made out that the banner had torn and part of it had been carried away, while what was left of the banner was whirling and banging about in the air, and, every few moments, hitting the steel pole holding it like the thump of a slap to the face. Then came the noise of running feet, and the rest of the deck watch hands were all scurrying down from the bridge deck almost at the same moment. In a few minutes they had the banner lowered and secured and returned back to the bridge deck to continue their watch. Then Pinter and Lynton went aloft to see where the torn part of the banner had gone. It was there, as the captain looked up at them that he astonishingly shouted, "Look, look there behind you."

Lynton and Pinter turned, and before them, hovering about in an undulating fashion, was a dark figure. It was the same figure she had seen on deck, sitting in the chair beside her. This time, he

     J. Wayne Frye

disappeared before her eyes, as she stared in bewilderment.

Pinter, heart pounding furiously, looked down at the captain as he shouted. "Deny that captain. Deny seeing what we saw."

It was no more than 2 or 3 seconds that the three on deck observed the dark shadow hovering above them, but it was long enough to finally make an impression on the captain. He said, "Don't be impertinent, but yes, yes I saw what you saw, but for the safety and well-being of the passengers we must not reveal it to anyone."

All three agreed that it must be kept a secret, but finally the captain was in agreement that with the famous dynamic dynamo on board, it might well be prudent to thoroughly investigate these strange occurrences.

Lynton shared the fact that she had seen that mysterious figure before on deck sitting beside her, and that apparently she was the only one seeing him. Neither man questioned her veracity and the three parted ways for the evening, but for Lynton, the evening would have an even more freighting encounter.

Wearily heading back to her cabin, she went down a flight of stairs, and as she reached the bottom, she felt that someone or some thing was behind her. For some reason she did not turn, but simply said, "Who is there?"

To her surprise came a response in a raspy, whisper-like voice. "I am but a warning to encourage caution, for evil is afoot here."

Lynton & the Haunting
Of the HMS Wind Dancer

Lynton moved cautiously to her right and walked under the stairwell, never turning to look behind. As she stared intensely at the wall under the stairs before her, she said, "Then tell me please what evil lurks about, so that I may counter it in some way. I am familiar with these types of horrors, and I am not afraid of the un-dead dead."

Lynton could picture in her razor sharp mind the rough skeletal-like deeply furrowed entity's face based upon the dark shadow that was reflecting on the wall before her as a result of the dim lights lining the hallway. It was that same man who had sat by her on the deck. The thing was in the same tattered clothing, and the scratchy voice was not scary but seemed filled with sympathetic concern for the mischief that had become a part of the Wind Dancer's legacy. Slowly and methodically, the voice, with deep emotion simply said as Lynton watched it fade into oblivion, "Be wary and watchful, for you are all that stands between the light and the darkness. Somehow, you must escape this vessel before the evil is let loose and those who are unsuspecting but secretly know their destiny fall before the blades of those who rise from hell." Then the shadow dissipated.

Never revealing what had happened, Lynton; nonetheless, began to query the ship's crew about the strange occurrences, and, with her winning ways, elicited more information than she had been privy to before. The chief steward, who had been sailing for years on the ship said to her in strict

J. Wayne Frye

confidence, "I used to ask others who had sailed on this vessel about rumours of ghosts, but the funny thing was no one ever could tell me anything definite concerning these apparitions. They seemed always to know things, but when it came to putting the knowledge into words it was as if they found that the reality of what had occurred melted recollections away. They would all end up usually by saying that you saw things or just felt things, and then they would wave their hands vaguely, but further than that they never seemed able to pass on the knowledge of something strange which they had noticed about the ship. Still, there were unexplained deaths, insane ravings by some, and others who simply seemed to drift off into trance-like states. They got frightened and they saw things and they, more often, felt things. It was the feel of evil that was more frightening than what they saw. A common thread was the occasional shadows that seemed to be lurking about in unlit areas. The shadows never talked, just flittered about in a menacing way."

Lynton, unafraid and determined, followed her usual methods of making a thorough and exhaustive search to confront these entities of apparent evil, save that one shadow which had whispered to her under the stairwell. She did this with the most scrupulous care, but found nothing abnormal of any kind in the whole vessel. She examined every nook and cranny, every casement and bulkhead, every exit from the holds. These and many other precautions she took with precision, but at the end of an exhaustive search had neither seen anything nor found anything.

Then on the next day something truly unique happened. She was pacing the upper deck in silence with Pinter when suddenly he stopped and looked up and out at sea in an area just under the bridge. He glanced at the wind-vane near him, then ruffled his hat back and stared out intensely. He said, "Something is not right."

"What," pleaded Lynton.

He pointed toward a low beam under the bridge and said, "Look right near the far end of the bridge beam."

A perplexed Lynton said, "I don't see anything."

Almost pleading, Pinter said, "Look to the far right out at the eastern horizon I tell you!"

"I see it!" replied Lynton. "There is something on the deck, something just undulating in the darkness."

Pinter then, as he pointed to the left of the one shadow, said, "Look to the left about 10 metres. There is another shadow moving toward that shadow, and then look another 10 metres right. There is a third one."

The three shadows slowly congregated together, hovering, undulating and seemingly dancing in sinister preparation for something. In a flash, that something was apparent, as the three shadows moved swiftly toward Lynton and Pinter. A whirling wind seemed to engulf them; an icy chill overwhelmed the two as they reached out to embrace each other in desperation to keep from

     J. Wayne Frye

being swept backward over the railing into the swirling sea below.

Just as it seemed the end for them was at hand, Williams appeared on deck to their left. He shouted out, "What the…."

Those were the last words he ever uttered, at least to a live person, as the three shadows swirled to the left, encircling him, while Lynton and Painter dropped to the deck, exhausted from their fight to keep from being swept overboard. Williams was not swept overboard, but rather, he was bashed against a nearby bulkhead, his neck so broken that it had swivelled a full 180 degrees.

For nearly half a minute, Lynton and Pinter lay depleted of all energy just staring into the stone cold eyes of a dead man who still seemed to be pleading for mercy that never came. They slowly arose as the captain and two crewmen who had observed what happened scurried down the upper deck stairs, while a curious rattling and vibrating noise aloft that sounded faintly above the hum and swirl of the now increasing wind could be heard. The noise was coming from three dark shadows aloft. It actually sounded like laughter of sorts.

Bending over the dead body, the captain shouted, "Williams, Williams!"

Lynton said, "Dead men don't answer."

There was silence among them all then. Suddenly, up aloft, there sounded a frightful scream. The next instant, something fell out of the darkness onto the lower deck. It was a heavy body that struck the deck near the confounded five people who were now near panic. With a gurgling, ringing, wheezy sound that sickened all of them, the deck steward Johnson was struggling for his last breath that never came. For the space of several seconds, there was again a dead silence among the crew; and it seemed to Lynton that the wind had in it a strange moaning note.

The captain barked orders for the bodies to be removed to the cold storage bin below deck, and that nothing about what had occurred should be uttered to the passengers. Lynton, growing weary of attempts to cover up so many deaths, said to the captain, "It is wise not to frighten the passengers, but maybe not prudent for their safety."

The captain, finally realizing the danger for his passengers and crew, without hesitation, replied, "Fortunately, the late hour assures the passengers were all asleep, and not one of them is likely to know what has happened. Please, dear lady, do not breathe a word of what has occurred. I will see to it that all precautions for safety are taken with due haste."

"I shall not divulge what has happened, I assure you," offered Lynton.

A more contrite, amenable captain replied, "Thank you, and I hope that I can rely on you and your unusual skills to help find an explanation for all this?"

Sighing, the dynamic dynamo replied, "I always try, but often there simply is no explanation."

 J. Wayne Frye

Chapter 5
Won't You Spare Me Over Another Year

*Thus, with the rising of the sun
Was the noble task begun,
And soon throughout the ship's bounds
Were heard the intermingled sounds
Of the dynamic dynamo as she plied
With vigorous determination on every side;
Plied so deftly and so well,
That, as the shadows of evening fell,
Her commitment was multiplied,
By not waiting for time and tide!
She could sense a coming trial ahead,
And wondered how many more would be dead.*

There was truly little Lynton could go on to solve a perplexing dilemma, but it did not take long for a new scenario of darkness to emerge. She was talking to a man named Stummer, who had been on the Wind Dancer for many voyages, about what he had seen over the years. She finally came right out and said it. "Do you think this vessel is haunted?"

"Ain't haunted," said Stummer. "Leastways, not like you mean."

Lynton, her interest piqued, said, "Go on."

He continued his pause, as though trying to grasp some elusive thought. "Things is queer, and it's been that way for a long, long time from what I have seen, from the very beginning when this ship was being built. I ain't one to gossip, but this here captain ain't putting all he knows on the table."

"Why do you say that?"

"Just some queer things he's been seen doing. Why he sits in his cabin all alone most of the day, and when somebody goes in there to take him coffee, a meal or ask for orders, they just see him sitting there staring."

"Staring at what?"

Shaking his head, Stummer replied, "You got me missy. He ain't much for talk no matter where he is or what he's doing. He is a morose sort. Yet, sometimes, he's been seen lurking about late at night in the hallways, seeming to be hiding in areas where dark shadows flitter about. He just knows somethin' he ain't telling. I once was on deck with him when he was just staring out to sea, and it was obvious somethin' was a bothering him, so I asks him what's the matter. He just says that shadows are coming. I looked out where he was looking but didn't see nothin'. Strange sort I tells you – a strange sort."

　　　　J. Wayne Frye

The feel of doom permeated within Lynton. Waves rose in intensity as the ship began to rock and roll. Lightning flashed all about in the sky, but there was no thunder heard following it.

The conversation had slacked off, as they both felt moody and shaken, no doubt, both reflecting on troublesome thoughts. Suddenly, Lynton heard the captain shout from directly above, "Stummer, get to the bridge."

"Aye, aye, sir," he dutifully responded and walked away as the captain gazed at Lynton, a quizzical look upon his face as he turned and walked back toward the bridge.

Lynton heard footsteps behind her and turned. Pinter stood before her and said, "Strange, but the captain is just roaming about, ignoring his duties on the bridge. He seems preoccupied about something."

"Who's at the wheel?" She asked him, in astonishment.

"The second mate," he replied, in a shaky sort of voice. "He's waiting to be relieved. I'll tell you all about it as soon as I get a chance. Gotta go below and check on an engine problem."

Lynton bade him goodbye and started toward the stairs to the lower deck. She passed two passengers and offered greetings but, as usual, got no response. She started down the stairs and noticed the captain now below, standing by the railing talking with someone. How had he gotten passed her without her noticing? There had been something queer happening, but what?

Presently, the captain left the dark-glad person to whom he was talking and commenced to walk the side of the deck. Once he came right aft, and, stooping down, peered under the wheel-box; but never addressed a word to Lynton who was now perpendicular to him, strolling along the same way as he. Some time later, he went down the weather ladder on to the main-deck, turning once to look back at Lynton, but still not saying a word. Directly afterwards, Pinter came running up to Lynton.

"I've seen it again!" he said, gasping with sheer nervousness.

"What?" Lynton said.

"What else? An infernal dark shadow," he answered. Then he leaned in closer to her and lowered his voice. "It came up from the lower deck very deliberately, up out of the darkness."

"Go on," she said.

"The second mate sent me to the bridge. "After that," he said as he nodded his head forward, stopping his words and just staring.

"Yes," plodded Lynton.

"Well, I'd been there about ten minutes, or a quarter of an hour, and I was feeling rotten about Williams, and trying to forget it all and keep things on an even keel, and all that; when, all at once, I happened to glance toward the lower deck, and there I saw it at the top of the stairs. I didn't know what to do. The second mate was standing forward and looking in a different direction. I was too aghast to say anything to him. I felt as if I were frozen stiff. The thing floated upward toward the bridge, coming towards me. I let go of the wheel and yelled 'look' at the second mate. He caught hold of me and shook me; but I was so jolly frightened I couldn't say a word. I could only keep on pointing. He kept asking me 'Where?' And then, all at once, I found I couldn't see the thing. I don't know whether he saw it. I'm not at all certain he did. He just told me to damn well get back to the wheel, and stop making a fool of myself."

"You're quite sure it wasn't thinking about Williams made you imagine you saw something?" Lynton said, more to gain a moment to think, than because she believed that it was the case.

"I thought you were going to listen to me, seriously!" he said, bitterly. "If you won't believe me, who will? You are the famous demon hunter. Tell me what it all means. What is this horrible thing? You know something, and I believe you're afraid to tell anyone, for fear it will cause a panic. Why don't you tell me? You needn't be afraid of my not believing you."

He stopped, suddenly. For the moment, Lynton said nothing in reply. He implored her with words of contempt. "Don't treat me like a kid, Lynton!"

"I am sorry," she said, with a sudden resolve to tell him everything. "I need someone to talk to, just as badly as you do. Someone whom I can trust, and I do believe I can trust you."

"What does it all mean, then?" he burst out. "Are they real? I always used to think it was all a yarn about such things, just silly old sea tales.

There are so many of them. I never believed in ghosts or the supernatural, but I have never encountered anything like what goes on here with this damnable ship."

"I'm sure I don't know what it all means, Pinter," Lynton answered. "I'm just as much in the dark there, as you are. And I don't know whether they're real, as we consider things real. You know that I saw a queer figure down on the main deck several nights before you saw that thing up here. It was not a menacing figure, just an old man, an indistinguishable character that sat by me. It was as if it was just there waiting, waiting for me to somehow recognize it, and then I saw it twice later, the last time below decks near my cabin where it spoke. It whispered to me that I should be wary and watchful, for I was all that stood between the light and the darkness. It said that there was an evil waiting to be released on this ship, an evil that would bring about doom. It seemingly intonated that I should somehow get off this ship."

Looking at her quizzically, Pinter said, "You mean that there is some catastrophe coming before we make port?"

"I am only telling you what I heard, nothing more and nothing less."

Sighing, Pinter said, "I can't get Williams off my mind. He was my friend, and I just wonder what he, if anything, saw before he tumbled to his death. The look on his face was as if he saw something horrible."

          J. Wayne Frye

Lynton & the Haunting
Of the HMS Wind Dancer

Lynton, ever the socially conscious muse, said, "In a world ruled by greed, the poor see horror every day, the horror of an economic system that keeps them in chains to serve those at the top. Here, on this ship, we see the same kind of evil, an evil of unmitigated horror purely for evil's sake. The evil here is palpable, and it has been let loose by an unknown force that, like the evil of capitalism, wants to crush compassion. There is an evil afoot that is every bit as insidious as the evil of greed, for it seeks to destroy, to devour, to consume souls in a feeding frenzy to satisfy an unquenchable appetite."

"Can it be stopped," asked a concerned Pinter.

Lynton, in a contemplative tone, replied, "Evil has never been stopped, only waylaid for awhile. I am afraid, like capitalism, it can never be destroyed, only stymied, but then it always rises again, rises from hell to consume, devour and destroy."

"You think then that there is some sinister plot, a plan for evil developing on board this ship, a plan that may actually destroy us all?"

"I do. Williams' death seems almost contrived, as if he knew it was coming. I never shared it with anyone, but he told me on deck once that he felt as if he was doomed. He said that it was like he had been on this voyage before, as it appeared he was going through a play, a practice of sorts for something."

Pinter stood contemplatively; silent, morose, moribund, as if he had the weight of the world on his shoulders. He took a very long deep breath and sighed. "You know what Lynton? I sometimes feel the exact same way, feel as if this is all a kabuki dance play practice, a prelude to some catastrophic event."

Lynton, a bit surprised, reflected back on her talk with Williams, the talk she had shared with no one, the talk that she had filed away and nearly forgotten. "That is funny you would say it that way, because those were the exact same words used by Williams to describe his feelings to me. His exact words were, 'a kabuki dance play practice.' That is very strange."

Dumbfounded, Pinter stood in silence, as did Lynton. Several seconds passed before Pinter said, "He told you that and now he is dead."

"Yes."

Again, sighing, Pinter said, "This ship is haunted. We both know that."

"Maybe, but there are different types of hauntings, different types of the supernatural."

"What do you mean?"

"Well, I've formed a bit of a theory that seems wise one minute, and lunacy the next. Of course, it's likely to be all wrong; but it's the only thing that seems to fit in with all the horrible things that have happened."

"Go on," he said, with an impatient, nervous movement.

"I scarcely know how to put it; but, if I'm right in what I think, it's the ship herself that's the real crux of the problem."

        J. Wayne Frye

"What do you mean?" he asked, in a puzzled voice. "Do you mean that the ship is haunted or not?"

"Wait until I've finished what I was going to say."

"Go on, then."

"About that thing you saw tonight," Lynton continued. "You say it came toward the bridge, up onto the upper deck?"

"Yes," he answered.

"Well, I am beginning to think that some of these things are not staying on the ship, but rather visiting the ship from the sea. My idea is that this ship is open to be boarded by those things. What they are, of course I don't know. They look like men in lots of ways. But what kind of men would rise up from the sea? I know it sounds silly, but I have seen so many unexplainable things in my life, I have a very open mind. I don't know whether they're flesh and blood, or whether they're what we should call ghosts or spirits."

"They can't be flesh and blood," Pinter interrupted. "Where would they live? Besides, that first one I saw, I thought I could see through it. And this last one seemed almost transparent, too."

"So are ghosts according to most people," Lynton answered. "But I am absolutely not saying they are flesh and blood; though, at the same time, I'm not going to say straight out they're ghosts, not yet, at any rate. I think they might be scouts."

"Where do they come from?" he asked, in a stupefied manner.

"Out of the sea," she told him. "I believe they are a vanguard, scouts for other entities!"

"Then why don't other vessels have them coming aboard?" Pinter asked. "How do you account for that?"

"Why do I believe that this ship is open, as I've told you - exposed, unprotected, or whatever you like to call it. I should say it's reasonable to think that all the things of the material world are barred, as it were, from the immaterial; but that in some cases the barrier may be broken down. That's what may have happened to this ship. And if it has, she may be naked to the attacks of beings belonging to some other state of existence."

"What's made this ship like that?" Pinter asked.

"I am but a sojourner on the path of learning. Perhaps something to do with magnetic stresses; but I am a layman when it comes to science, and this is likely way beyond my deductive abilities and understanding. Anyway, I suppose, inside of me, I don't believe it's that. Maybe I am grasping at straws in an attempt to explain something that is unexplainable. Sometimes evil is a result of pure rottenness, the kind of rottenness that is prevalent in a world where the rich prey upon us peons and never reach out with compassion. Maybe this ship is just rotten like that, rotten to the core, and within it is an evil that attracts more evil. Think about how people with money only associate with others who have money. Maybe evil is the same way; an evil ship attracts evil entities that prey upon the unsuspecting, prey upon those with little

     J. Wayne Frye

to fight off that evil. Like the poor who cannot fight against the evil of those at the top of the economic ladder, perhaps those of us on this ship are unable to stand against the evil of this vessel and the evil of the entities that inhabit it. Perhaps, there may have been some rotten thing done aboard her. Or, again, it's a heap more likely to be something quite outside of anything I know can even be contemplated."

"If they're immaterial then they're spirits?" Pinter questioned.

"I don't know," Lynton said. "I have to accept that there are things I cannot explain, but here we are on a ship the likes of which I have never even considered before." She reached into her pant pocket and brought out her ticket. She waved it in front of Pinter, and continued. "This was sent to me by my husband, who wanted me to have a relaxing journey." Then she laughed, put the ticket back in her pocket and with a smile said, "He would be livid if he knew I was once again tackling supernatural phenomena."

Then, Pinter said something that would come back much later to haunt Lynton. With longing eyes and trembling voice, he said, "You know, it is like all this has happened before. I feel as if I am, as mentioned earlier, in some type of play, a kabuki of malevolent evil that is not going to be satisfied until everyone on board this ship is dead."

Lynton observed several passengers meander by, seemingly lost in thought. Their clothes were unusual, but she could not figure in what way. They stood out for some reason.

As she watched a couple walk by arm-in-arm, she said to Pinter, "Have you noticed that the passengers seem distant and uncommunicative?"

"That is the norm for our passengers, Lynton. This is not a jolly ship. It is not a place where merriment prevails. The captain wants to protect them from knowledge of anything suspect, but the truth is these people are already in a pit of despair. There is no happiness that abounds on this vessel. There is no capacity for it. There seems to be no laughter from our crew and from the poor passengers. I believe all suspect the evil, suspect that this is a damned voyage."

"You are indeed observant my dear Harold. I have noticed that since first coming aboard. You know, even before I came on board, I had turned around to leave the ship out a feeling of extreme doubt that I should board her. I do not know whether I imagined it or not, but I could swear I saw a thin as a rail deckhand urging me with a wave to turn back and board. When I was taken to my cabin, I felt as if I was being led to a tomb. I noticed the steward who escorted me said nothing, but he had a quizzical look, a look that seemed to be asking why I was foolish enough to board this vessel."

"I remember asking myself that of you. I wondered why you would be on this ship. Still, I am glad you are here, because you are a ray of sunshine in the darkness. Please go on with your

        J. Wayne Frye

explanation of your theory. I am curious, so curious."

"It's so hard to say what I really think, you know. I've got a queer idea, that is just forming, an idea that seems a bit preposterous, but I cannot get it out of my mind."

"Go on," Pinter said.

"Well," Lynton replied. "Suppose the earth were inhabited by two distinct kinds of life. We're one, and those shadows we see are another. My husband wrote a book about one of my adventures called *Lynton Viñas: Shadow in the Darkness.* I will not bore you with the details, other than to say, I encountered a shadow before, and it was trying to communicate with me, but these shadows do not seem to desire any communication, save the one who cornered me below decks the other night. Rather, they seem bent on doing pure evil, even murder,"

"This is fascinating. Go on." Pinter said.

"Well. Don't you see, in a normal state we may not be capable of appreciating the realness of the other state? But they may be just as real and as material as we are. Ordinarily, we would be on two different plains, but somehow, here on this ship, things have somehow gotten crossed. It is as if we are interfering with their space."

"I am following you, yes. Please continue."

"Well," Lynton said. "The sea, the ship may be just as real to them, as to us. I mean that it may have qualities as material to them, as it has to us; but neither of us could appreciate the other's realness, or the quality of realness on the sea, on this vessel. Ghosts, spirits or whatever, they recent their space being invaded. Does this ship always take the same course both back and forth?"

"It does, never varies a degree on the compass. The route is always exactly the same."

"There is something about the ship and something about the captain, something about everyone on board, crew and passengers alike that just seems out of the ordinary. I cannot put my finger on it, but it is there. It is palpable, so palpable that you can feel it, but I am unable to explain it. There is an atmosphere that somehow makes it possible to see what maybe should not be seen. There is something that is giving us power to see and feel things that we ordinarily would not. I believe the same applies to them. They are able to see things they would not ordinarily see. What they see is us, and that may be frightening them so much that they are resorting to violence. They may well be as frightened by us as we are by them. The adherence to the same course voyage after voyage may have them annoyed, may have them upset that this evil ship keeps invading their space."

"Then, after all, you really think they're ghosts, or something of that sort?" Pinter said.

"I suppose it does come to that," Lynton answered.

"I think you ought to tell the captain about this," he said. "If it's really as you say, there are precautions that maybe could be taken."

        J. Wayne Frye

Lynton & the Haunting
Of the HMS Wind Dancer

"The captain's attitude has adjusted, but not changed. He is not going to really do anything," Lynton replied. "Even if he believed it all; which we're not certain he would, there is something he is hiding, something that seems to prevent him from taking concrete action."

"Perhaps not," Pinter answered. "But if you can not get him to believe it, things will never be safe."

"I know that, which is why we must be eternally vigilant. There is something I am missing, and I know it. It is something that is as clear as the nose on my face, but I just cannot figure it out. It is like I have a light on in my head, but it is too dim for me to really see."

Then she took out her ticket from her pocket again and held it up. "This is more than a ticket on a ship. It is a ticket that has opened up a doorway to the macabre."

She put the ticket back in her pocket, took a deep long breath and said in a soft reverent voice, "My husband recites a poem that is very apropos to our situation."

"Oh death! Oh death! Oh death!
Won't you spare me over till another year?
Please, please I have much still to do.
Well, what is this that I can't see,
With ice cold hands taking hold of me?"

"Well, I am death, none can excel,
I'll open the door to heaven or hell.

Lynton & the Haunting
Of the HMS Wind Dancer

I'll fix your feet till you can't walk.
I'll lock your jaw till you can't talk."

"I'll close your eyes so you can't see.
This very hour come and go with me.
In death I come to take the soul,
Leave the body and leave it cold.
To drop the flesh off of the frame.
The earth and worms both have a claim."

"Oh death, Oh death! Oh death!
Please I beg of you in all my fear.
Won't you spare me over till another year?
Won't you spare me over till another year?"

Sighing, Pinter said, "Death has been this ship's companion for far too long. You know I feel like all this is just a constant repeat of something that has happened over and over."

Philosophically, Lynton said, "Despite all that has occurred, there seems no panic among crew or passengers. There is a calm resignation among them all. It is as if they are waiting for something, waiting for the evil to manifest itself."

Pinter hung his head low and then looked up, then back down at Lynton. He said, "There it is."

Not raising his head, but cutting his eyes upward toward the top deck, it was obvious what was there. Lynton very slowly tilted her head upward and there was a dark shadow looking down at them both. Lynton thought, "Oh death, oh death, oh death, won't you spare me over another year."

     J. Wayne Frye

Chapter 6
You are Something Else, Lynton Viñas

*With all its terror and mystery,
The darkness so like unto death,
Portended the coming doom
In the silence of twilight gloom.
And for a moment one might mark
What had been hidden in the dark.*

*Day by day, the vessel's mysteries grew,
And there was the dynamic dynamo so true,
Who toiled to find the ghosts at length,
Never for once not showing strength.
Where there is trouble Lynton stands tall,
For before evil she has great gall!*

Lynton was strolling the upper deck when she got a fright. Looking down at the lower deck, she could have sworn that she saw Williams at midday walking near the railing. No, it could not be, just her imagination she thought. Poor fellow! His death had been so sudden. All day the ship's crew and passengers were exceedingly gloomy despite the semi-cloudless day. Then, about noon, it happened. A mist, a dark gloomy mist descended upon the ship.

When Lynton first noticed it, like everybody else aboard, she took it to be some form of haze, due to the heat of the sun peeping through the clouds. The wind had died away to a light breeze, and Lynton was standing on the promenade deck with Seaman Warren Walton, who said, "Looks as if we gonna get a bit of light rain. Them clouds is darkening. It's gettin' quite hazy," he said in a surprised manner.

Lynton glanced up quickly. At first, she could see nothing. Then, she saw what he meant. The air had a wavy, strange, unnatural appearance; something like the heated air over the top of boiling pot with just a bit of steam forming.

"Mighty strange looking," offered Lynton.

"Ain't common, ma'am. Ain't never seen a mist like this 'un."

Suddenly, the whole ship was covered in a thin haze, as the sun and horizon disappeared.

"Weird," Lynton said.

"Yes," Walton lamented, looking round. "I never seen anything like it before, not in these here parts."

"Heat wouldn't do that?" asked Lynton.

"No," Walton replied.

Walton went on with his work again, occasionally exchanging an odd word or two.

Lynton started to turn and leave. She noticed the stolid expression on Walton's face had changed suddenly to a look of complete surprise. He opened his mouth very, very slowly and formed the words with caution. "By gum!" he said. "It's gone."

Lynton looked all about. And so it had, the mist had all dissipated. She stared at Walton, and he stared at her. On the upper deck, Pinter had come out. He looked down at the two of them and immediately shrugged his shoulders, indicating his mystification over the situation.

"Well, if that don't beat it all," exclaimed Walton.

Lynton made no reply; for she had a sudden, queer feeling that things simply were not right. She, in no way, could shake off the feeling, as she took a good long look out to sea. She had a vague idea that something was different. The sea looked brighter, somehow, and the air clearer, but her mind was still foggy. She thought and thought. She felt she had missed something; missed something that someone had said or done that would alter her perception of things. It played over in her mind again and again. What had she missed? What was she seeing but not seeing?

Yet, the rest of that day she could not come up with anything specific. Only when the evening came and she saw the mist rise faintly and the setting sun shining through it, dim and unreal, that she realized what she had missed, but she was not ready to accept it yet.

Lynton & the Haunting
Of the HMS Wind Dancer

As the night wrapped itself around her like a blanket, not warm and comforting, but cold and foreboding, she shivered on deck in anticipation of what lay ahead. The rest of the day, the haze would descend on the ship for awhile and then disappear. At that time, no one seemed to think very much of the matter. Apparently they assumed it was just another anomaly among many anomalies that had become common place. And when Lynton mentioned the haze to the captain, and asked him whether he had noticed it, he, in a dismissive manner, shrugged his shoulders, and only remarked that it must have been heat, or else the sun behind the clouds drawing up water. She let it stay at that; for there was nothing to be gained by suggesting that the thing had more to it. Then, as dark night approached, something happened that set her wondering more than ever, and showed her how right she had been in feeling the mist to be something unnatural. She was on the upper deck, peering out at sea and pondering the events which had placed her on what apparently was a truly ill-fated voyage. Unlike the norm, the night sky was perfectly clear now, not a cloud to be seen, even on the horizon. It was hot, standing at the railing; for there was scarcely any wind, and she was feeling drowsy. Walton was down on the main deck with the men, seeing about some job he wanted done. There were no passengers strolling any of the decks. How strange Lynton pondered, as the entire voyage, most passengers, except for an occasional sojourn to the lounge, where they

 J. Wayne Frye

seemed to huddle in groups and whisper quietly to one another, simply stayed in their cabins, stayed there as if they were waiting for something. Waiting for what, thought Lynton.

Presently, with the heat, and the moon beaming right down on to her, she glanced round in search of a passenger, any passenger. There simply were none. She looked down into the water where the waves seemed to beckon her, beckoning her to dive overboard and feel their coolness. It was thus, as she fought the overwhelming urge to jump, that she came to see something altogether surprising and mystifying, a full-rigged ship with huge dirty grey sails, closing in on the port side. It looked like something out of the 1800's. Her sails were scarcely filled by the light breeze, and flapped as she lifted to the swell of the sea. She appeared to have very little way through the water, certainly not more than a few knots an hour. Away aft on this incredible sight, hanging from the last yardarm, was a string of flags. Evidently, it was signalling to the Wind Dancer. All this she saw in a flash, and she just stood and stared, totally astonished. Where had this ghost ship come from, as in the light breeze and a clear night the ship should have been visible for hours before total darkness. Yet, she could think of nothing rational to satisfy her amazement. There she was, but how had she so suddenly appeared? How had the ship come there without her seeing it before?

All at once, as she stood, staring, she heard a noise behind her. She turned and no one was there.

Then, she turned back to have another look at the strange ship; but, to her utter bewilderment, there was no sign of her, nothing but the calm ocean, spreading away to the distant horizon. She blinked her eyelids a bit, and pushed the hair off her forehead with a smooth brush of her right hand. Then, she stared again, but there was no vestige of the ship, and absolutely nothing else unusual, except a faint, tremulous quiver in the air as the now darkening surface of the sea seemed to be lapping forward to the distant horizon.

Dumbfounded, she stood there alone on the deck of a ship that had six hundred passengers. Where were they? Why did she seem all alone on the ship? What kind of passengers paid good money for a voyage and then simply spent most of the time holed up in their cabins?

Mystified with a growing fear of what was happening, she searched around the sea for any sight of the strange vessel, but there was nothing. Where had the ship gone?

As she stood contemplating, she had another thought, or, perhaps, an intuition and she asked herself seriously whether this disappearing ship might not be in some way connected with the other queer things. It occurred to her then that the vessel she had seen was nothing real, and, perhaps, did not exist outside of her own brain. She considered the idea, gravely. It helped to explain what was becoming the unexplainable. Had the ship been real? She felt sure that among the others aboard, surely there must be some other

     J. Wayne Frye

passengers about who had seen it. But she saw no other passengers at all. Where were they? Then, abruptly, the reality of the other ship came back to her. Yes, it was real. She knew it was, because she remembered how the ship shifted about on the open sea, and how the sails had flapped in the light breeze, and how the string of flags fluttered as it cut through the water. She had been signalling. Signalling for what reason?

She pondered, wondered and pondered again and again. She had reached a point of irresolution, and was standing with her eyes focused on the sky to the aft of the ship. She desperately wanted reassurance that she was not seeing things, and perhaps forming incoherent thoughts as a result of all the strange occurrences. .

All at once, as she stared, she seemed to see the ship again. It was farther in the distance to the aft of the Wind Dancer now, but, yes, it was there. It was definitely there. It was only a glimpse she caught of her, dim and wavering, as it was in a mist far behind. Then the ship grew indistinct, and vanished again; but Lynton was convinced now that it was real, and had been in sight all the time. She had just somehow lost sight of her.

That curious, dim, wavering appearance had suggested something to her. She remembered the strange, wavy look of the air just before the mist had surrounded the ship. And in her mind, she connected the two. It was nothing that strange really. The strangeness was with the Wind Dancer, itself. It was something that was happening aboard her. It was evident that the other ship had been able to see the Wind Dancer, as was proved by her signalling. In an irrelevant sort of way, she wondered what the people aboard of her thought of the Wind Dancer's apparently intentional disregard of their signals. The captain and those with him on the bridge must have seen her, but they were not indicating so.

After that, she thought of the strangeness of it all. Even at that exact moment, the other ship could see them. She knew it. And as she glanced up at the bridge, she wondered why those there could not see the other ship. She could see them looking out of the bridge windows, and apparently seeing nothing of the other ship. The whole ocean obviously seemed empty to them. How could they ignore an ancient sailing vessel on the sea behind them?

Strange thought Lynton, as she reflected on what was happening and more appropriately on what had happened. She felt a kinship with Pinter and Walton, but even they exhibited an uncertain strangeness about them, as if they were also hiding something. Then, a fresh thought came to her. The Wind Dancer was seemingly sailing a solitary course, out of the normal shipping lanes. Consequently, they were on a course that would avoid the sightings of other ships. And, for the most part, there was the constant darkness caused by continual cloud cover, with only intermittent clear skies. In her mind, the last glimpse of that ship coming up from behind came back to her in vivid detail. And, she had a curious thought that maybe she had looked at her from out of some other dimension. Maybe that ship was unable to see the Wind Dancer. Maybe that ship was from another time and another place. For awhile, she deeply contemplated the mystery of the idea when suddenly she felt someone shaking her arm, and she realized she had drifted into a near trance. The captain, shaking her said, "You are asleep on your feet. What's the matter with you, woman? You look like you were about ready to jump over the railing."

Lynton turned toward him and just stared into his craggy, weather worn face, without saying a word. She seemed incapable of actual, reasoning speech. Words were forming in her brain, but not coming out her mouth. Finally, she managed to utter, "I,I,I."

"Speak up, speak up. What is it? Come on say it, spit it out."

Sighing, Lynton said, "You would not believe me if I told you."

"Try me."

Tepidly, Lynton replied, "I was looking at that ship away to the aft. She has signal flags up."

"What?" He said, cutting her short with disbelief. "What ship?"

He turned, quickly, and looked aft. Then he wheeled round to her again. "There's no ship!"

"There is captain." She responded. "It's out there following us. I saw it – an old sailing ship, looked like one from maybe from the 1800's."

"You gone balmy?" he shouted. Then, he was silent. He came a step towards her and stared into her face. It was obvious he did think she was a bit mad. He shook his head and walked away.

Pinter walked up, and shaking his head, said, "From the look on the captain's face, you must be upsetting him again."

"I told him there's a ship aft, signalling us with flags," she said.

Looking back over his shoulder, he said, "There's no ship out there."

"There is, or there was I tell you."

"Well, look for yourself now. Do you see anything?"

Perplexed as she looked diligently for something that was no longer there, she bowed her head and sighed as she said, "Harold, you are my grasp with sanity – you and Walton. Yet, I feel that you and he are not 100% honest with me. There is something you are holding back. Have you ever seen an old five mast sailing vessel on any trips on the Wind Dancer?"

He got a quizzical look on his face as he said, "No, I have not, but there are tales of a ghost ship, a ship that has sailed these waters for hundreds of years, a vessel that appears out of nowhere and will shadow other vessels from a distance. However, you must remember that we are on a route that is rarely traveled anymore. The Wind Dancer prowls these waters like a ghost ship itself, and I have often asked the captain why we do not chart a course along the more utilized routes that other vessels follow. His response is mysterious at best. He just intonates that this is the course the ship has always followed, and there is no reason to change it after all these years."

Still, Lynton was not satisfied that Pinter was revealing all he knew. She let it go, because she saw no need to press it at the time. He bade her farewell and went back to his duties.

She paced slowly to and fro thinking about that ship, the mist, and all the strange things that had happened. Her thoughts drifted toward the obstinacy of the captain. She thought of him as a pig-headed old fool, until it occurred to her there might be some method to his obstinacy. She realized that she should never have told him about the ship trailing them. What good had it done, other than to solidify his view of her as a fool?

She ceased to bother her head about him, and fell to wondering why Pinter had been dismissive of her ghost ship tale. Did he guess more of the truth than she supposed? And if that were the case, why had he refused to listen to her, going off for what he said were his duties. Those duties had never kept him from conversing with her before.

After that, she reflected about the mist. One idea appealed to her very strongly. It was that the actual, visible mist was a materialised expression of an extraordinarily subtle atmosphere, in which the ship was moving. Was the ship moving through some unknown astral plain?

Abruptly, as she walked backwards and forwards, taking occasional glances over the sea her eye caught the glow of a light out in the darkness that had now descended on the ship. She stood still, and stared. She wondered whether it was the light of a vessel. She saw then that it was undoubtedly the green light of a vessel off the port bow. It was plain that the ship was headed right in front of the Wind Dancer, toward the bow. What was more, she was dangerously near, the size and brightness of her light showed that. Instantly, she looked up at the bridge where the captain was peering out. She frantically motioned toward the ship, so that he might see it if he hadn't already. Surely, she thought, he has already seen it.

The captain waved his hands in a quizzical manner as if asking what the problem was. He shook his head as he looked in the direction to which Lynton was pointing.

As the captain shook his head, Lynton thought that he must be blind. It was obvious the ship was going to ram them. Or was it? Lynton turned back to look again, and the ship had disappeared. She ran forward and leaned over the rail and stared, but there was nothing, absolutely nothing except the darkness all about. For perhaps a few seconds she stood bewildered, and a suspicion swept across her that the whole business was practically a repetition of the affair in regards to the trailing ship. She did not doubt the fact that, there was a vessel ahead, and very close ahead, too. Her only hope was that, seeing the Wind Dancer was not getting out of her way, she had slowed and waited. Then, all at once, she heard steps coming along

    J. Wayne Frye

the deck and a seaman shouted, "Captain wants to know what is going on with you. Is there something he should know? He is all discombobulated about what is going on."

"There's a light off the port bow, headed our way, or there was one. I am sure."

"I was on the watch until sent to check on you. Ain't seen no lights. None of us have seen any."

"I don't know," Lynton answered. "I've lost sight of it myself. It was a dim light, like maybe from a lantern, about a couple of points on the port bow. It seemed fairly close."

"Perhaps their lamp's gone out," he suggested, after peering out pretty hard into the night for a second or so.

"Perhaps," Lynton said, not telling him that the light had been so close that, even in the darkness, they should now have been able to see the ship.

"You're sure it was a light, and not a star?" he asked, doubtfully, after a long stare.

Not wanting to make a case of it, she just said, "Maybe so. Maybe that was it." She didn't believe it, but what use was it to belabour the point with people who were beginning to think she was crazy.

He left and went back to the bridge. Lynton stood staring, and something came to her mind as she looked around. Why were there no passengers out? Why were they never out strolling the deck? It was rare to see any of them.

She stared out into the blackness, and there it was again, the light headed their way. It was broad on the bow, and told her plainly enough that she had to run aft to avoid the coming carnage. She did not wait a moment; but sung out to the bridge that there was a dim light about four points off the port bow headed their way. The light did not seem to be more than about a couple hundred feet away. She thought to herself that surely the bridge hands would see it now. Alas, the light faded and then disappeared.

The same seaman was by her side again, asking "What the devil is your problem now?"

"It was there I tell you, ready to crash into us."

"Ma'am, I think you need to go to your cabin and get some rest."

Pinter walked up and dismissed the seaman with a wave as he said to Lynton, "What's this about you seeing lights? Maybe you could point out to me where you saw them."

This she did, and he went over to the port rail, and stared away into the night; but without seeing anything. Lynton, almost frantic now, practically pleading, said, "Well, it was there I tell you. It was. I've seen it twice now - once, about a couple of points on the bow, and this last time, broad away on the bow; but it disappeared both times, almost at once."

"Doesn't make sense," said Pinter. "Are you sure it was a ship's light?"

"Yes! It was a dim light. It was quite close."

"I don't understand," he said again as he tuned and continued, "I'll go up and get the spy glasses. Be right back."

She looked up at the bridge and saw Pinter and the captain in what appeared to be a frantic discussion. Arms were waving and heads frantically shaking.

In less than a minute, he was back with his binoculars; and, with them, he stared for some time at the sea to the left and right. All at once he dropped them to his side, and faced around at Lynton with a sudden question: "Where is it then? If she's shifted her bearing as quickly as all that, she must be precious close. We should be able to see her easily, or at least that infernal light."

"It is queer that it has disappeared."

"Yes, I am inclined to think you just imagined it," offered Pinter, who had never questioned Lynton's veracity before.

She was puzzled by his change in attitude toward her, but realized that there was something bothering him, something that he had not shared as of yet. She did not press it, as she said, "I saw it, pure and simple."

"O.K., I believe you," replied Pinter, as he put his binoculars to his eyes and scanned all around the darkness. He walked a bit aft, stood by the port rail for perhaps a minute before taking another look around with his binoculars. Then, without a word, he went down the lee ladder, and away aft along the main deck.

"He's jolly well acting strange," Lynton thought to herself. Still, she could not understand why he had suddenly taken a more distant approach to her. Was it because she had shown no interest in his obvious amorous intentions? She stood and contemplated if he had any idea about the truth of what was going on. Was he privy to some dark secret about what was happening?

She was walking about the lower deck in deep thought, feeling defeated in her search for answers, when she saw that infernal light for the third time. It was very bright and big, and she could see it move about in the darkness. It again appeared to be very close.

She looked around the entire lower and upper decks and wondered why the passengers were never out and about. It was a calm, moderately mild night. Why did they all seem to stay in their cabins or the main lounge? She even considered going into the lounge to grab a passenger and ask if they could see the light. For half a minute, she watched the light in the distance. It was no longer near the ship. She was not going to take her eyes off it this time, and there was no sign of it disappearing. Every moment she expected Pinter to appear so she could hopefully show him the light. He didn't.

Finally, she saw Warren Walton staring down at her from above. She shouted up at him, "Dim light off the port beam."

As she shouted the words, the light blurred and vanished. It immediately appeared again, and then just as quickly, immediately disappeared again. She stamped her foot and very nearly swore. The thing was making a fool of her she thought as Walton said, "See no light, Lynton."

She bowed her head and said, "Of course not. Never mind."

Walton looked around at the dark sea. "Sorry missy, just don't see no light. Maybe it is some kind of reflection from the ship's cabin lights."

"No," Lynton said. "It's gone. It's come and gone three times now."

He looked intensely and silently at her in the darkness. "Missy, if I was you I'd have me an early rest tonight. Go to bed and get some shut-eye. There's nothing' like a snooze when you get weary and start seeing things out on the ocean. Been that way a time or two myself."

"What?" she said with an indignant tone.

"It's all right. You'll be all right in the mornin'. Don't ya worry about it." His tone was sympathetic but dismissive. She did not like it.

She walked away, leaving Walton without a word. "Sleep," she thought. "How am I going to sleep after seeing what I have seen?" She wanted to talk to Pinter, wanted to maybe ask him why his change in demeanour.

She searched both decks but could not find him. She walked to her cabin, sat down and felt a rising anger that she was unable to discern the truth about what was going on. She felt tired, angry and miserable. She went over and over in her mind what had occurred. She could not understand why no one else saw the lights.

There was a shuffling sound outside her door. She got up, went over and opened it. She stared up and down the hallway but saw nor heard anything.

Still she could not bring herself to close the door, as she just stood there staring, almost as if expecting something to happen, something that might shed some light on the mystery that was perplexing her.

Suddenly, at the end of the hallway, under the dark stairwell, she saw that old man in torn, dirty, dilapidated old clothing who had sat bedside her on deck. He was just standing there, a dark shadow-like figure, seemingly waiting. Waiting for what she wondered? Was he waiting for her, waiting for her to move down the hallway and confront him?

She did not have time to do that, as suddenly to her left, out of a cabin came Seaman Johnson. What was he doing in a passenger cabin she wondered as she pointed toward the far end of the hallway and pleaded with him, "Do you see him?"

Looking at her extended right arm, scanning it with his eyes all the way to the fingertips and then peering down the hallway he asked, "See what?"

The man was gone, gone in the blink of an eye. She, again, almost pleaded. "He was there I tell you. He was there."

Johnson nodded his head slowly, keeping his gaze fixed on her face. "I believe you Lynton. I believe you – don't fret. I didn't see nothing, but I believe you."

Almost to the point of crying with joy with his affirmation of belief, she took a deep breath with the realization that this man understood more, perhaps, than she had hitherto thought, something that he actually wanted to share. She asked a simple question. "What's going on with all the subterfuge? Why are so many people avoiding the obvious fact that there is something unusual, maybe supernatural, going on here?"

"Didn't nobody believe you about the lights, right?" he asked.

"Yes," she replied. "I was told I was imagining things."

"And what did you say?"

"What could I say?"

"Why didn't you blooming well ask Walton and Pinter if the captain weren't imagining something when he sent several of us crewmen chasing after some old shadowy looking man in ragged clothes?"

"What? You've been looking for the man I just saw at the end of the hallway?"

"Probably, I was just in that there empty cabin checking for him. I was sent down here to check all empty rooms to see if 'un we got us a stowaway."

Lynton, a sense of relief that she was not imagining things, said, "You think it was a stowaway? You really think that?"

"It might have been a stowaway, you know. You can't say as it's ever been proved it ain't."

"You don't believe that do you?"

Ignoring her question, he said, "So it was suggested you get some sleep, uh? I think that was all a big bluff."

"What do you mean, bluff?" Lynton asked.

He nodded his head. "Everybody knows you saw that light, just as much as I do."

Elated, Lynton said, "Then you and others don't doubt that I really saw it?"

"No doubts little lady, no doubts at all."

"I am so relieved, so relieved to know I am not balmy. Still, this whole business is queer I tell you."

"There are a lot of other damn queer things happening aboard this vessel. Things none of us can understand - things that just keep a happening on voyage after voyage. You know we keep hearing stories about how people sign on this ship, take a voyage or two and disappear to never be heard from again, but I swear I been on many a voyage on this here ship, and most people I work with been on here again and again. It is almost like they can't free themselves of this here ship. It's like, like, well like they can't get off her for some reason. It just ain't natural I tell you. Not natural."

Suddenly a voice could be heard above decks, calling out, "Light off starboard bow."

"There you are," said Lynton with a jerk of her head. "That's about where I spotted the light. She couldn't cross our bows, so she up helmed, and let us pass, and now she's hauled up again and gone to our stern."

Looking at her night gown, she realized it would be inappropriate to go above in that attire. She said "Wait a second," went inside and quickly put on a pair of pants, tucking her night shirt in and returned to Johnson with a determined look, as she

 J. Wayne Frye

blurted out, "Let's go above and see what is going on."

As they stepped out on deck, she heard the second mate shouting out, away to the aft, to know the whereabouts of the light. He seemed frantic.

She looked at Johnson and said, "I believe the blessed thing's gone again."

They ran to the starboard side and looked over; but there was no sign of a light in the darkness astern. They were perplexed.

The second mate, looking at Lynton in her pants and tucked in night gown, obviously was enjoying the skimpy nature of the gown, but managed to say while staring at her, "I can't say I see any light anywhere now."

Lynton and Johnson had no reply. They both headed toward the starboard rail. Another seaman was standing there and said, "Where's that light gone to? It was right there I tell ya," he said as he pointed into the darkness. He then cupped his hands around his eyes, shielding any superfluous light from the sides as he concentrated on finding the light.

"You did see it, sailor? You did see it?" asked Lynton.

"I did. Yes, I did. It's the darndest thing I ever come across. The light was there in plain sight and the next second she were gone, clean gone."

Lynton turned to Johnson. "There's proof of that light."

"Well," he said. "I'll admit I thought maybe we were both a bit balmy. I thought you might be mistaken; but it seems you did see a light. Yes, you did."

Away aft, they heard the sound of steps along the deck. Pinter, Walton and the captain came running up. They seemed out of breath and bewildered.

The captain, looking unsettled that Lynton was there, addressed the seaman while staring at her bodacious body in the partial moonlight, "Where is this infernal light?"

"Gone," replied the seaman.

"Gone!" the captain said. "What do you mean?"

"She were there one second, sir," replied the perplexed seaman, "and the next second she were gone I tell ya. She were just gone,"

"That's ridiculous," the captain replied. "You don't expect me to believe that do you?"

"I am telling ya what I seen, sir. That is the full-on gospel truth."

"And how many others saw this light?"

"Several sir, several."

Lynton looked at the captain with a satisfied smirk and said, "And me, of course, little old me has seen it before."

The perplexed captain, obviously rattled, looked the alluring Lynton up and down. The situation was nerve rattling, but apparently not nerve rattling enough to altar the typical male response to a sensual-looking young woman. He was perturbed and his demeanour showed it, despite his interest in Lynton's appearance. "My guess is that all of you have been listening to this little troublemaker here. She's putting things into your heads. What the devil's the matter with you all that you've taken to this sort of game? You know very well that you saw no light! This woman here has you all dumbfounded with her tales of lights, shadows, ghosts, whatever."

The captain turned to leave, looked back over his right shoulder and told them all, "Back to your posts. This light business is over." He then, as he left, without looking back said, "I actually fell for your blarney woman, myself, but have come to my senses. And Ms. Viñas, you'd do us all a favour if you went to your bed like the rest of the passengers and stayed in your cabin the rest of the voyage."

She did not reply out loud, but whispered to herself, "Yeah, that ain't gonna happen, and you know it."

As they all departed, save Lynton and Pinter, he took a deep breath and said, "Been several men reported seeing a light that was clear for awhile and then disappeared. So, there is definitely, or at least was, a light out there. You are not imaging anything. It is real, or maybe at least real in the minds of those who have seen it. You do not deserve to be treated with disdain. Why, at one time the captain even wanted you to help. I was there when he asked you, but now he is back to his old self, back to casting doubt on you. I apologize for my apparent slights previously and my curt manner. There is something going on I cannot get my head around, and I am afraid that I took it out on you. I should not have done that, but, you see, there is something completely off kilter here. Strange things have happened on this vessel before, really strange things, but there is a difference this trip, and I think they are different because of you." He then took a long, obviously prurient scan of Lynton's body, which made her feel uncomfortable.

Used to that type of interest from men, she looked him directly in the eyes, as she said, "I appreciate your obvious interest, but I am married, very married. Remember that, and remember that there is a more pressing matter than the titillation of your libido."

"I'm sorry. I'm sorry. Forgive me."

"Nothing to forgive. It is a compliment, and perfectly natural."

With a broad, jocular smile, he said, "You are something else Lynton Viñas."

Chapter 7
Begging for Mercy When There Was None

*There is something deep in the hold
Strong as youth, and as uncontrolled,
Paces the things restless to and fro,
Up and down so very bold.
Spirits that are not at rest;
That roam at whose behest
With ceaseless, unending flow,
And quietness as silent as falling snow.*

*On the deck, another evil does abide,
Standing silently by someone's side.
Shadows from the flags and shrouds,
Like the fluttering cast by the clouds,
Broken by not even a light's fleck,
Falling around them on the deck.*

*Do the entities know the chart
Of each and every sailor's heart,
All its pleasures and its griefs,*

Lynton & the Haunting
Of the HMS Wind Dancer

All its shallows and rocky reefs,
All those secret currents that flow
With such resistless undertow,
And lift and drift, with terrible force
A ship that must complete its course.

What happened after the last light escapade brought home pretty vividly to Lynton, if not to any of the others, especially the captain, the sense of personal danger aboard. It was now obvious.

She had gone below and her last impression of the weather was that the wind was picking up. There had been a great bank of clouds rising astern, which made it look as if it were going to breeze up still more. The next morning, she got up early and took a jog around the lower deck. As usual, no passengers were up at 5:00 AM. She could tell at once, as the cold morning sea air slapped her in the face, that there was a storm brewing as she had postulated. At the same time, she heard the voices of the men on the watch.

On the upper deck, she could see faintly through the morning fog two seamen checking to make sure the lifeboats were secure. Nothing seemed out of the ordinary. Yet, she could sense from the tepid nature of the men securing the lifeboats and the hushed whispers of the other hands on deck that something was not right. There was a queasiness about them which transposed itself to her. She stopped her jogging and looked up at the darkening clouds. She felt the need to return to her cabin and did.

     J. Wayne Frye

Back in her cabin, she could not shake the feeling that there was something new amiss on a ship that had plenty amiss already. It was nearly 6:00 AM and she felt the uncontrollable urge to return to the deck when she peered out her window and saw in the morning mist that light, that infernal light that had caused so much trouble. It was not too far in the distance and headed right for the ship. She felt an urgency to get on deck.

Most of the seamen were assembled on the main deck, lining up for morning inspection. As they stood there, Lynton noticed that from the upper deck, right above the bridge, a baton on one of the lifeboats she had seen the men securing had worked its way loose and was dangling right over the men assembled by the bridge. This was a small enough matter in itself, and yet really terrible in its consequence to one of the men assembled. She was about to call out, when it happened. A big gust of wind swept over the ship as she saw a dark shadow sweep over the lifeboat. The baton flew into the air and in the blink of an eye something crashed to the deck with a slogging, horrible thud. A seaman's head had nearly exploded as the baton crushed his skull. He never said a word. He just died.

For a second, all there, including Lynton, stood in utter shock. So shocked were they that there was no rush to the seaman's side, just momentary bewilderment at the suddenness of what happened. Then someone bent over the fallen sailor, looked up and said, "He's dead!"

The next instant, they must have seen the light heading toward the ship as they scurried, leaving the body lying there, to the port side railings where the light, in the morning mist was moving slowly toward the ship.

The captain, appearing on the deck as if he simply materialized out of thin air, shouted, "You have a comrade down you uncaring blokes. Get over there and assist him."

By this time, Lynton had climbed to the upper deck where the captain was shouting. She looked directly at him and said, "Nobody's going to help that man. He was dead the instant he hit the deck, and there will be a lot more dead unless something is done about the strange things happening on this ship. One of those strange things is that light the men are looking at. That light is headed dead on for this ship."

The captain walked toward the men, who parted as he went to the railing. Peering into the morning mist, his shock made Lynton realize that he was seeing the light, too. She moved beside him and the light disappeared as a dark shadow suddenly jumped skyward, rapidly moved over the crowd assembled there and turned to zip toward the seaman lying on the deck. It descended upon him and just hovered there for a few seconds. A bluish light seemed to emanate from the body's mouth and merge with the dark shadow. The shadow absorbed the light completely and whisked back out over the crowd into the morning mist, disappearing in the vastness of the ocean.

    J. Wayne Frye

Suddenly, from aloft, by a lifeboat, a frantic cry of "help, help" could be heard.

"Captain," Lynton shouted as she pointed at the upper deck.

"Help, help," shouted the man over and over. He was pleading now, as everyone looked up the stairs toward the sound. The words pounded into Lynton's head, as he continued to shout, "Oh god, oh god, please help! Please!"

Nobody could see the man calling out, only hear him. His desperation was obvious.

"Look," shouted Pinter, as he pointed to the far side of the upper deck, where the back of a man could be seen, obviously a sailor. He was fighting with a thin dark, shadowy figure.

Abruptly, Walton's voice struck in. "Up there. Up there," as he pointed toward where the melee was occurring. He sprang, along with a couple of others, up the main stairs to the upper deck.

Several other men started to go, but the captain said, "That's sufficient numbers. Stay here the rest of you." Then he turned to Lynton and said, "Especially you."

Lynton, never one to cower before authority, simply said, "I'm going," as she bounded toward the stairs.

The men were all racing like fiends toward the sounds of the beleaguered sailor. The morning dark haze was so thick it prevented Lynton from seeing any distance in the darkness; but, at the point from where the sounds were emanating, what appeared a titanic struggle was taking place.

"They're fighting," shouted Walton as he rushed ever forward.

Abruptly, there came again a wild crying from the darkness. A strange, wild medley it was of screams for help, mixed up with violent, breathless curses. Walton stopped, turned to Lynton and said, "Stay back."

She ignored him and proceeded with three other men in his direction. The heavy foggy dark mist up there was so think one could not see hand in front of face. She reached Walton, and as she looked into the darkness she saw a straggling, flickering ray of a light off in the distance. She also saw something dark and hulky-looking that clung, struggling, stumbling, menacingly to the sailor. Walton plunged towards it with fists flailing while the seaman had his right arm tightly around a railing; while with the other, he appeared to be fending himself from something on the other side of him. At times, moans and gasps came from him and sometimes curses. Once, as he appeared to be dragged partly from his hold, he screamed loud at Walton pleading for help. His whole attitude suggested complete despair. As Walton flew at the dark figure, along with the seaman, Lynton and the others seemed to stare at the melee without actually realizing that the affair was really happening.

During the few seconds which they had spent staring and breathless, Walton had moved around behind the dark figure and was pounding away at it relentlessly, but how do you fight a ghost?

          J. Wayne Frye

The other men were preparing to enter the fray, when Walton shouted, "Stand back, stand back and get me a flash light, so I can see this creature face-to-face," as he finally, along with the seaman, had a fierce hold on the attacker.

A sailor with a huge flashlight shined it toward the combatants so that it lit up the leeward part of the deck. The light showed through the darkness, as far as to where Walton struggled so weirdly. Beyond him, nothing was distinct.

It seems impossible to convey truly here the terror felt by all there as they confronted this dark figure of a thing. Walton's head craned forward as he tried to get a better look at the assailant in the shifting light of the huge flashlight, but still, the mist only allowed the outline of a dark shadowy thing.

The captain had made his way onto the deck and spoke, abruptly. "Hold that miscreant. Hold him well, I tell you. Walton, Walton do you hear me?"

"Aye, aye captain, holding fast here."

"Keep a tight hold. Tight I tell you. I want to see this bastard."

"We got him, captain," said the seaman.

The captain reached the seaman and put his hand on his shoulder, with an unlikely soothing gesture. "Steady son now, steady. All is OK."

At his touch, as though by magic, the young fellow calmed down, while the captain continued, "Hold him tight boys, hold him tight. This is no ghost. This is flesh and blood, I tell you. Yes sir, this is flesh and blood if ever I saw it."

Just then, Walton said, as a heavy jacket dropped to the deck, and he and the seaman were left holding thin air, "Damn, nobody's in this jacket captain. Nobody I tell you."

"There ain't nobody here," the seaman shouted in total bewilderment.

Lynton saw something shadowy at the extreme end of the deck, by the lift. Its dark penetrating eyes stared. It stood perfectly still on the deck, and she saw that it was the figure of what looked like a man. It grasped at the lift, and commenced to swarm up, quickly. It passed diagonally above the crowd's heads and reached downward with a boney arm and hand at the captain.

"Look out!" Lynton shouted. "Look out!"

"What is it?" he called out, in a startled voice. At the same instant, his cap went whirling away out into the mist. He suddenly looked up as Lynton pointed above his head, and the dark shadow just hovered there. Then, in an instant, it flittered away out to sea.

All there were aghast with fear, but the captain, maintaining his calm said, "Come now men. Come, and we will go below and reflect on what has occurred. This is bewildering."

They all went willingly enough, though without saying a word. They seemed like mystified children. They shivered, shook their heads in disbelief, but said nothing.

The captain, on the lower deck, asked the seaman what happened above. All he could say was that a dark shadow engulfed him, and he felt a

        J. Wayne Frye

fear that he were being smothered. He was shivering and shaking, as he talked.

Meanwhile, the seaman who had been struck in the head was moved into cold storage, another victim who would have to be accounted for to the authorities when the ship arrived in Lagos. The authorities were going to have their hands full for sure investigating this, thought Lynton. Then she thought of her husband, Wayne. "Oh my," she said to herself, "he is going to call me his little headache again and chastise me for another perilous adventure. How do I get myself into all these misadventures?"

Lynton noticed, as she looked aft, that the captain had moved to the back of the deck now, contemplatively leaning up against a bulkhead. He looked worried; but was silent as Walton stood by his side seeming to also be deep in thought. Pinter was busy with a couple of sailors whispering orders. Then he turned to one, as the others left, evidently telling him something; but his tone was so low that Lynton caught his words only with difficulty. It struck her that he seemed pretty subdued after all the excitement. She got parts of his sentences in patches, as it were – "broken," she heard him say. "And the Dutchman," she heard the sailor reply, "I've seen it."

"Two, straight off the stern, three in," offered Pinter.

The sailor said, "yes."

"Of course, you know … accident," Pinter went on.

"Is it?" the sailor said, in a tepid voice, as he glanced at Pinter in a doubtful sort of way.

After a moment's hesitation, Pinter said something further, that she could not catch; but there seemed a lot of concern in his voice and manner.

The captain appeared on deck, went over, bent in close and whispered something to the two. He straightened up and glanced back at Lynton. There was a certain niceness in his action as he nodded at her as if to say, "Hey, you are OK."

Suddenly, the seaman who had been talking to Pinter whizzed around, and stared at her as though she were a ghost. Pinter turned also; but before he could speak, the captain took a step towards her and said, "You alright? That was a pretty scary episode."

"I'm OK," she replied. "Thanks for asking."

"I'm glad to hear that," said the captain, seeming unusually genial. He turned towards the aft; walking away slowly. Pinter smiled at Lynton, said nothing, turned and walked with the captain. They were whispering something to one another. The seaman, after a quick glance at her, followed them. It occurred to her like a flash that the three men had stumbled upon a portion of some truth in the whole previous episode. It was evident that, in their minds, they had connected some dots in the perplexing puzzle of what was going on, but they were not going to share what they knew with her. She recollected the fragments of the remarks she had heard between Pinter and the seaman. Then,

     J. Wayne Frye

she reflected on those many minor happenings that had cropped up many different times, and even her nominal friend Harold Pinter had seemed unwilling to share all he knew about the strange occurrences past and present. She wondered whether they were beginning to finally comprehend the significant connections, their beastly, sinister significance, and were avoiding telling her what they knew out of fear that she would somehow bring her considerable detecting and demon hunting skills to bear on something they did not want exposed.

Abruptly, her thoughts jumped to the vague future before all aboard. She began to wonder why she had seen no one on board with a cell phone except her. There were not even any of the crew with one. Why, she wondered, reaching down to grasp her own phone and quickly getting on Facebook in hopes she could talk to her Wayne, because he was too stubborn and too cheap to have a cell-phone. He said that they were modern ways of distracting people from face-to-face communication, trapping people in the downward spiral of authoritarianism where corporations and the wealthy kept people distracted from discussing how everyone was being made slaves to technology, so that in the end, they would also be slaves to the moneyed class that kept them occupied with the mundane while they garnered more and more of the economic pie so that they and their progeny could continue the modern feudal system that he equated to slavery.

She could not get a connection. She thought, as the mist closed in around her, that it was the atmospheric conditions. If she only knew the truth of why she could not get a connection, but that would come later.

She took a deep breath and noticed a passenger at the far end of the deck. She had made little attempt to communicate with any of them after being ignored by that old man in tattered clothing at the beginning of the journey, because, frankly, she saw them all as disinterested in any conversation. Somehow, they all appeared lost in personal thought and even appeared to be avoiding her, as if she were an interloper into their little world on the vessel.

The man, standing by the railing, had on what would have been fashionable in 1968 Canby Street London. He had a stylish Sassoon haircut to match the outdated clothing. He even had penny loafers on. Just as she approached him, a young woman of equal tasteless fashion sense, with bright red hot pants and a psychedelic blouse strolled up and took him by the arm, gazing, with him, out into the morning mist.

"Tom," she said.

As she spoke, several spots of rain fell, and Lynton glanced up at the sky. It had become thickly clouded now, and was merging with the mist.

"Looks as if it is going to breeze up," she said, as they both ignored Lynton, who had stopped and was leaning on the railing near them.

"Yes," he replied, without looking at her, still staring into the mist.

Several crew members came strolling by, but never looked at the couple or Lynton. It was nearly 7:00 AM, and all was quiet. Only the two passengers and Lynton were on-deck, and Lynton, eavesdropping on the pair found their conversation interesting, as the man, Tom, said to the woman, Celeste, "You know, it seems that this is our loneliest voyage yet. How I long for it to end."

"It is an endless voyage of heartache it seems," offered Celeste.

"It has been the longest voyage, yet, a voyage that seems to have no end, ever. How I long for the tranquility of being on land again, off the rising and ebbing of the waves that seem to never stop, never allow for a respite from the eternal motion of this damned vessel," Tom said in a low, raspy, melancholy voice.

They were a strange pair thought Lynton, as she turned and went starboard. She saw several crewmen, and one of them, apparently in charge, said to the others, "Come on now, lads. Make a move. It's got to be done. Same as always, same routine again and again."

They all seemed to just be going through a routine, a routine that was as old as time itself, as old as the first time men sat sail on the sea. She followed their mannerism with glee, watching them perform on-deck duties that they had performed so many times before, but she was astonished how robotic they all looked. She had fully expected them to look up at her, as all men usually did, but they did not. The robotic motions made her feel alone, as there was no recognition of her whatsoever. Then, one of the men looked at the sea, then back at Lynton and stared at her intently while saying, "What's the matter with you?"

"Nothing," she said, as a seaman came up behind her, and it was obvious the question and the stare had been addressed to him, not Lynton. It was as if none of the men even saw her standing there.

The man behind and to her right walked forward and answered the question by saying, "Nothing wrong with me."

Lynton could sense the sailor was lying, and later she would know it, because she would soon hear men crying and begging in unison, begging for mercy when there was none.

Chapter 8
Make Us Suffer This Again and Again

Fore, behind and all around,
Floats and swings the horizon's bound.
Seems at its distant rim to rise
And climb the crystal wall of the skies,
And then again to turn and sink,
As if heading the outer brink.

Ah! It is not the sea;
It is not the sea that sinks and shelves,
But something within that must rise
With endless and uneasy motion,
Now touching the very skies,
Sinking into the dark depths of ocean.

Ah! If souls but poise and swing
Like the compass in its brazen ring,
Ever level and ever true
To the toil and the tasks sailors do.
Shall they sail until they reach

Lynton & the Haunting
Of the HMS Wind Dancer

That dark and lonely beach?

The things they see, and the sounds they hear
Will be those of foreboding, evil, dark fear.
Dark fluttering shadows dance about there
Where nothing will ever be serene or fair.
This is a sombre cruise lost in time,
Where death rings again its chime.

Lynton, in her lonely quest for answers stood in silent thought watching the men go about their tasks. The captain came among them, and they all nodded good day in robotic unison. He neither offered recognition to them or to Lynton. He went and stood by the railing, looking into the thick foggy mist. Lynton walked across to the starboard side, as she heard the captain sing out to the mate in charge of the crew.

"Call all hands to shore-up the lifeboats on this deck, immediately," barked the captain.

"Very good, sir," the mate replied. Then he raised his voice and shouted to two of the men, "Go forward Monte and Bob, and make sure those boats are secured."

"Aye, aye," they shouted back.

Lynton continued to walk away, but for some reason stopped by the bulkhead, looked behind the stairwell and heard two sailors talking in muffled tones. "I tell you," said one, "I ain't walking that deck on watch tonight. I just ain't gonna do it."

The other sailor replied, "Don't blame you after what happened."

     J. Wayne Frye

Lynton & the Haunting
Of the HMS Wind Dancer

They saw Lynton and one of them said, "Hope you ain't reporting what you heard ma'am."

Winking and smiling, Lynton replied, "I haven't heard a thing, but what happened?"

"Ma'am, its better you don't know, but if you just gotta know, if you want the real skivvy, go below to the bunk house and talk to Jacobs. He's the one with a curtain over his bunk."

Lynton went below to the bunk area, walked though the empty room toward a back bunk that was blocked off with dark curtains. They were drawn, so she whispered, "Can I open the curtains and talk. It is Lynton Viñas. I think you know of me."

"Go ahead," was the whispered response.

He was lying on his back, breathing in a queer, jerky fashion. She could not see his face plainly, but it seemed rather pale in the half-light.

"Jacobs," she said, "what happened to make you go down below decks and lie down in your cot? Two sailors told me you could enlighten me about something queer that happened."

"You that famous demon hunter, ain't you?"

"Well," replied Lynton, "I don't know how famous I am, but yes, I have been called a demon hunter in a few adventures I have had over the years."

He was breathing heavily now, and Lynton feared for his welfare. He looked ill. She leaned in and said, "Please tell me, tell me what has laid you low here. Is it that you are sick from a disease, or sick from fear?"

His eyes got misty as he said, "It's fear I am ashamed to say. Yes, it is fear."

He began to shake and quiver as he whimpered, "What are they doing? What are they doing? Can't you see?"

Lynton reached down and shook his leg in an attempt to get him out of his stupor. But at her touch, Jacobs became more enraged and began to shout in a frightened voice, "Help! Hel...!"

"Quiet, quiet," Lynton softly urged.

Yet, he only cried out the more. And then, abruptly, she caught the sound of a frightened clamour of men's voices, near the door. There were curses, cries of fear, even shrieks and above it all, someone shouting, "I'm through I tell you. Ain't going above decks no more."

Lynton turned and moved toward the men, giving up on getting any answers from Jacobs. She pleaded with the men, "What happened?"

One of them shouted, "Walton is gone. This dark shadow descended onto the main deck and plucked him right up, plucked him into a dark whirlwind and off it took him, off into the mist. Disappeared completely did he. They's all looking for him now, but we ain't doing it. We ain't taking a chance on being whisked away ourselves. Don't care if they charge us with mutiny. They can go ahead and do it, rather be in jail than be dead. I tell ya. Yes sir, take us to jail with a smile on our faces. Yep, better alive in jail than dead, absolutely. Good thing all the passengers are still in their cabins."

One of the other sailors piped in, "Strange how you don't never see no passengers on deck. Nobody ever comes on deck, excepting that couple, that strange couple is up there sometimes. Rest of the passengers just hides out in their cabins most of the times. Only comes out to go to the main lounge on occasion. Strange it is, strange."

Lynton made her way through the men and headed for the upper deck, determined to ferret out what was behind the latest incident. As she walked out onto the upper deck, the mist had become darker and thicker with the haze almost being black. Something gripped her waist from the rear. She made a desperate clutch for the stair railing to her right and it was well for her that she secured the hold so quickly, for the same instant, she was wrenched at with a brutal ferocity. She said nothing, but lashed out into the greyness with her famous right foot that was part of what Wayne Frye had coined in numerous books, "the high heels from hell." Only she had no heels on this time. Still, her sneaker glad right foot was lethal. She could not categorically say with certainty that she struck anything as she was too desperate with surprise, and yet, it seemed that her foot encountered something soft, that gave under the blow. It may have been nothing more than an imagined sensation; yet, she was inclined to think otherwise; for, instantly, the hold about her waist was released; and she commenced to scramble down onto the deck, sprawling there for a second.

Lynton & the Haunting
Of the HMS Wind Dancer

As helping hands assisted with her raise from the deck, in a blind whirl of excitement the crowd of shouting, half-crazed sailors asked if she was alight. In a confused way, she was conscious that the captain and Painter were among those assisting.

"What was holding onto you?" asked Pinter.

"I have no idea," replied Lynton. "All I know is that it had a fierce grip, but at the same time it felt slight of body. Did none of you see it?"

They all shook their heads negatively, and one sailor said, "Only a dark shadow was what I saw, and it was almost transparent."

Among them there came a moment of dead silence, and Lynton noticed the wail and moan of the wind aloft. Suddenly, the captain blurted out, "We have to find Walton. Leave no place unsearched."

There was a moment's pause. Then one of the men spoke, "How do we find him, sir? How do we find someone grabbed away by a swirling dark shadow?"

"Who saw him last?" the captain asked.

One of the seamen stepped forward into the light that streamed through the lounge doorway. He had on neither coat nor cap, and his shirt seemed to be hanging about him in tatters. "It were me, sir, I think. Yes, I am sure I was the last to see him, because whatever it was came for me first, came right for me. It had me in its grasp, and then as Walton came up, it let me go, and in the blink of an eye, it had him, took him away in a whirlwind."

     J. Wayne Frye

Pinter, who was standing near the sailor, took a pace towards him, stopped and stared intensely as he said, "Where did you last see that whirlwind, where?"

He pointed at the upper deck. "Up there, up near the stairs. It hovered there, but I could not see Walton, it was too dark, too much mist about."

The captain said, "Pinter take three men and go up there. The rest of you search this ship in every nook and cranny."

The captain turned to two seamen and said, "Go to the bridge locker and get some heavy duty flashlights, now."

They were back in a flash, handing the lamps to the four men, who headed up the stairs. Lynton started to follow them, but the captain reached out and held her arm. She gave him a stern look and he released it, knowing that arguing with her would be fruitless. She followed the four men to the upper deck.

Fearless Lynton trailed behind the men with the bold memory of that horrible clutch that held her so determinedly, and knew that if her husband knew of this cavalier disregard for danger, he would have a mild fit of anger that she was being so bold. As he always said, "whatever happens to you happens to me. If you are hurt, I am hurt. Your pain is my pain."

"Come! Come," Pinter said. "We can't leave Walton to an uncertain fate in the hands of those abominable creatures, whatever the hell they may be."

Lynton & the Haunting
Of the HMS Wind Dancer

The men were bunched up, and Lynton stood right behind them with intensity and determination. Pinter said, "Now, I know none of you are cowards, but be vigilant and careful. We must stay together. He then looked back at Lynton with a protective glare and continued, "You Lynton, come up front and stay behind me. The rest of you surround her."

She could have protested, as she was an equal to any man in bravery, but she did not. Rather, she accepted his chivalry with gratitude. One of the men blurted out, "Sir, what sort of a thing is it we are looking for?"

There was silence from Pinter. Lynton could not resist answering. "We are looking for a supernatural phenomenon, something that has apparently risen from the bowls of the earth, from hell if you will, and my guess is that there is more than one of them. These are creatures of darkness that apparently feed on fear, feed on the susceptibility of the living to an amalgamation of evil that has, for some reason, decided to descend upon this vessel and feast on its souls."

Pinter reached out and touched Lynton's right arm, as if to say, "Enough, please don't frighten the men more than they already are."

Not a single man there wavered, though. They had true grit; and Lynton was astonished at their complete devotion to duty, to searching for a missing colleague. Yet, she was to have even a greater astonishment; for, abruptly, the captain appeared.

 J. Wayne Frye

He stood there with a gun in his hand. He handed it to Pinter and said, "Use it if necessary."

Lynton did not bother to tell him that against these creatures it was her estimation that a gun would probably be useless. She recalled the many times she had dealt with Americans, who had a love affair with their precious guns. Like them, apparently the captain saw guns, bullets and bombs as the answer to all problems.

The captain turned and walked away. Lynton whispered to Pinter, "A gun is useless against these creatures."

He replied in a low whisper, "I know, but it may well be a comfort to the men."

"Understood," replied Lynton.

"Now men" Pinter began, "this is no time for dilly-dallying. Lynton and I will go aft, and I want the rest of you to come along with us, and carry the lights high above your heads."

There was no hesitation whatsoever as the three men eagerly followed, while Pinter said, "keep those lights straight ahead of us."

As they approached the bulkhead, Pinter said to one of the sailors, handing him the gun, "Take this boy, and stand here to guard our rear. Any dark thing comes your way, blast it. We'll come running."

"Yes, Sir," answered the young sailor.

Pinter looked at Lynton, as if he wanted some type of guidance from someone who had dealt with these matters previously. She had the confidence of all there.

Lynton & the Haunting
Of the HMS Wind Dancer

On the obvious prompt for assistance from Pinter, she said, "As soon as Pinter and I move beyond the bulkhead, you two keep your torches concentrated in front of us, especially on anything that materializes. Be careful to keep your lights away from shining directly on us. Do you clearly understand?"

"Yes," said the men in chorus.

A sudden idea occurred to Lynton in regards to the nervous sailor with the gun, and she turned, and went back to him. With a look of deathly seriousness, she said, "Guns are rarely the answer to a problem, as so many wars and deaths have proved, but there can be no negotiation with these creatures. Whatever they are they do not seem to have the power of speech, and I do not believe a bullet will stop them, but a bullet can certainly stop us. Make sure you do not fire into the darkness, because you may well hit us. Fire the gun as a warning, not as a weapon. Do you understand what I am saying?"

Looking a bit doubtful, as he stood there holding the pistol, he meekly replied, "I do."

Pinter, the two sailors by his side and Lynton stood stark, determined, driven and unrelenting as bulwarks against darkness. They were as staunch as wild-west gunfighters who had strolled into the dusty streets at high noon to face down outlaws bent on destruction and mayhem. They were about to do battle in the arena of seafarers who had plied the oceans for generations unafraid, bold, dauntless and brave.

Lynton & the Haunting
Of the HMS Wind Dancer

Thus was the stage set for an epic battle between the dark and the light. And Lynton recollected some sage words of wisdom shared poetically by her dear husband about a ship caught in a vortex of evil in one of his books.

The sea is not calm on this terrible night.
The tide is full, the moon lies not fair.
Upon the ocean, there is an unknown light.
There are creatures in the night that stand,
Darkening and vast, with nothing to say.
Evil lurks all about on a doomed vessel.
The world there on it seems
Lies before all like a land of dreams.
So various, so dark, so new;
Hath no joy, nor love, nor light,
Nor certitude, nor peace, nor help for pain;
And all are there as on a darkling plain,
Swept with confused alarms of struggle and flight,
Where good and evil are about to clash by night.

Pinter, determined and sure, but still weary and cautious, led the way forward. As they went, the light from the flashlights made the fog seem to part where the beams of light struck. Still, the darkness in the middle of the day was so thick one could have almost cut it with a knife. And then, suddenly, as though the sight of the piercing lights had awakened Lynton to a more vivid comprehension, it came to her new and fresh, how strange was the whole business. She got a little touch of despair, and asked herself what was going to be the end of all these seemingly incoherent happenings.

Straight ahead, in the mist, Lynton could make out a dark figure over by the railing. She stepped lightly, as did the others; for fear that whatever was there would be alerted to their presence. The thing obviously had its back to the four interlopers.

"Careful," whispered Pinter, "shine all your lights on that thing."

All at once, two of the three lights unexplainably went out, went completely dark. Despite banging on them, they would not come back on. The thing before them did not turn but rather, by contrast, seemed to get darker than the surroundings. They all froze where they were, standing completely motionless. The one light still working, being held by Pinter, seemed no more than a sickly yellow glow against the gloom. Strangely, in front of that creature, from above, high above there wailed down through the darkness a determined cry.

A voice could be heard from above, the voice of the captain. "Get that light on the thing."

The penetrating light from above flashed onto the creature. "Smartly with that light, boy," the captain shouted. And the blue glare blazed out again, almost before he had finished speaking. None of the four standing there on the lower deck could see the captain or the men with him. Whatever the thing was in front of them, it did not move. It stayed perfectly in place, back to the four.

Then, suddenly, when the morning sun peeped through the clouds all there were aghast at the sight before their eyes. The entire deck in front of that large, hulking figure before them was filled with flickering, grotesque shadows cast by the dripping sunlight above. A group of the men with the captain became clear now and, like the four people below, they stood in shock, their faces sunken and pale and unreal under the gleam of the dim light as they focused on those things below, things that seemed to be feasting on something.

Slowly, the big hulking thing began to turn toward the four. The captain shouted from above, "Shoot it. Shoot it I tell you. No, shoot them all. Yes, shoot them all."

Pinter called for the seaman with the gun to come forward. He left his post and scurried to the front of the group, aimed and just as he was about to fire, Lynton shouted, "No, no, I think there is a seaman among those things. I see a seaman I tell you. It might be Walton. You may hit him."

The captain shouted, "Hold your fire."

Suddenly, the dark shadows converged with the big hulky one and they all fluttered about and then went over the railing into the sea. The sun went behind the clouds again and the mist and darkness closed in.

The captain shouted down, "See any signs of Walton?

"None," shouted back Pinter.

"Should have fired! Should have fired," retorted the captain.

As all stood dumfounded, the captain shouted into the darkness. "Walton, you there, man? You there? Speak up man if you are there. Walton, Walton."

They all listened intently; but nothing came to them beyond the blowing moan of the wind, and the lapping of the sea against the ship. Pinter climbed onto the railing, shining the now brighter flashlight into the dark sea in search of he knew not what.

By the light from Pinter's torch, the ocean looked vast and unyielding. And then, they heard a scream from behind. Pinter turned his flashlight in that direction and the seaman with the gun was gone, disappeared completely. A few seconds passed, and then the light from Pinter's flashlight streamed out as the wind began to howl. All there were in shock, and probably a full minute went by, and there was still no sign of the seaman with the gun. From above, the men with the captain shone their flashlights downward. As they all stood in bewilderment, a loud cry, a cry of pain was heard and onto the deck from high above in the mist, the gun dropped with a resounding thud. It lay there in the streams of light. It looked as useless as it was, just laying there as if it had been tossed from the hands of someone who saw it for the evil it was, an evil that brought death to the innocent as well as the guilty. It was the tool of the ill-informed, a tool used to instil fear, a tool of evil in a world where naked aggression was the norm, rather than the exception.

                    J. Wayne Frye

Then out from the mist-laden darkness at the starboard, there came a curse from a seaman, followed almost immediately by a noise of something vibrating.

"What's up?" shouted the captain. "What's up?"

The seaman shouted back, "There's something in one of the starboard lifeboats, something making it shake. It's vibrating, just vibrating like crazy."

"It's messing with the foot-rope, Sir-r-r!" he drew out the last word into a sort of gasp.

The second mate had come down from above. He bent quickly, with his flashlight, crouching as it were and signalling for Pinter to follow him. Lynton craned round the far side of the lower deck with Pinter by her side as the three scurried starboard.

The seaman by the lifeboat was shouting for help All at once, in the beam from the second mate's flashlight, Lynton saw that the starboard foot-rope attached to the lifeboat on the upper railing was being violently shaken by shadows. And then, almost in the same instant, the second mate shifted the light from his right to his left hand. He put the right into his pocket and brought out a gun. He extended his hand and arm, pointing at something a little below the swirling rope. Then, just as Lynton started to plead with him, a quick flash spat out across the gathered shadows undulating by the boat, followed immediately by a sharp, ringing crack. In the same moment, she saw that the foot-rope ceased to shake.

"Shine your light on the boat," demanded the second mate of Pinter.

"That's better, Pinter," shouted the second mate.

"What was it you were shooting at?" asked Pinter.

The captain shouted down the same question.

The second mate was speechless, and could not find words. He finally stuttered, "Damned if I know. It was just dark shadows."

Lynton sprung across to where the second mate and Pinter were standing. She gazed with intensity at the lifeboat, noticing a little round hole in the front of it slightly below the foot-rope, through which a ray of light shone. It was undoubtedly the hole which the bullet from the second mate's revolver had made.

To her right, Pinter was just staring as his flashlight seemed to be dwindling in power. She glanced at his face through the dark haze. He was paying no attention to her; instead, he was staring up above his head at the captain who had moved around toward starboard on the deck above them.

"See anything of Walton?" asked the captain, suddenly observing the area with intensity.

"Nope, nothing, nada," replied the second mate.

Lynton, observing intensely, was still looking at that hole in the boat. There was something surreal about it. Then, she said, "the seaman who was whisked away aft, pulled up into the mist. I think I know where he is. Not sure about Walton, but I think if you'll look in the lifeboat, you'll find the seaman with a bullet hole in him."

Just then, someone from behind shouted, "Found Walton, found him I say."

"Where?" barked the captain.

"There! There!" replied the sailor.

Lynton, now distracted from her concentration on the bullet hole in the lifeboat, looked up along the deck railing toward the rear. At first, she could see nothing; then, slowly, there grew upon her sight a dim figure crouching over something lying on the deck. She stared, and gradually it came to her that what was on the deck was a body that was only visible indistinctly.

"Walton. Walton!" the captain shouted out from above.

The sailor leaning over the body shouted up at the captain. "He can't answer captain. He ain't never gonna answer nobody again. Walton's dead."

Lamenting the death of a man with whom she had become friendly, Lynton turned back toward the lifeboat as she shouted to the captain, "There's another dead one, too, the sailor who was with us. Check the lifeboat and I can assure you he's behind that bullet hole in the boat."

The second mate, shaking with remorse that he may have accidently killed the sailor, moved to the lifeboat with great trepidation. He lifted the tarp, looked down into the boat with Lynton by his side. Sure enough, there was the seaman, dead.

The second mate, almost pleading, said, "I didn't know. All I saw was shadows, shadows I tell you."

Lynton, placing her hand on his right arm, said, "Look closely. Look at his face. You see the terror embedded in it. Believe me; you did not kill this man. Check and you will see no bullet hole in his body. This man died of fright, a fright that is burned indelibly into his face. Look I tell you, look."

Pinter joined him in examining the body, and sure enough, there was no bullet hole anywhere on it. As they concluded the examination, they shouted up to the captain, "Dead he is, killed by fright it looks like. This man saw something that literally killed him with fear."

Aft of the lifeboat, a loud thud was heard and then a dark indistinct shadow could be seen gliding down the aft railing. It was descending full upon the second mate, Pinter and Lynton as they stood by the lifeboat. Suddenly, every single flashlight faded and there was only the dark mist, nothing else. The second mate, now fearful of shooting in the darkness, kept his gun in his pocket, as the shadow moved toward them.

Down on deck aft could be heard someone calling. "Langley's dead. He's dead on the deck."

Above, the captain, unable to see in the heavy fog, shouted "Nobody move, stay still, don't move I tell you. Be calm."

Lynton thought to herself, "yeah, stay calm he says, but you don't have some dark shadow moving your way with assumed ill intent."

Pinter grabbed Lynton's arm, shouting for the second mate and the sailor to follow him. The trio

          J. Wayne Frye

did not tarry, just followed without question.

As the shadow moved slowly their way, they scurried to the stairs and bounded upward toward the captain and his men on the upper deck, just as the shadow reversed course and started back toward where the dead body lay and other sailors were gathering to remove it. The captain shouted at them, "Down, down on the deck, all of you. Play dead."

No sooner had the captain told the men to get down on the deck than from below came the sound of a man screaming. All above raced down toward the screaming.

Lynton caught a momentary glimpse of a man running from the doorway on the port side of the vessel. In less than half a minute they were upon the deck, and among a crowd of the men who were grouped around something. Yet, strangely enough, they were not looking at the thing among them; but away aft at something in the darkness.

"It's on the rail!" cried several voices.

"Overboard!" called somebody, in an excited voice. "It's jumped over the side!"

"There weren't nothing!" said the man who had come out the door.

"Silence!" shouted the captain. "Where's the first mate? What's happened?"

"Here, sir," called the first mate, shakily, from near the centre of the group. "It's Seaman Collins. The 19 year old, sir. He-he-."

"He what?" said the captain.

The mate hesitantly replied, "He's dead, sir."

"Let me see," said the captain, in a quieter tone. The sailors stood to one side to give him room, and he knelt beside the man upon the deck.

"Shine a flashlight here," the captain said as he knelt by the body.

The light was on a man. No, a boy who was lying face downwards on the deck. Under the light from the flashlight, the captain turned him over and looked down at a face that was etched with terror.

"Yes," he said, after a short examination. "He's as dead as a man can get."

He stood up and regarded the body a moment in silence. Then he turned to the Pinter, who had been standing by during the last couple of minutes. The captain said, "Eight total! Eight good men." He delivered the comment in a grim undertone that indicated a man with a heart, something Lynton had not been sure of before.

Pinter nodded stoically and cleared his voice. He seemed on the point of saying something; then he turned and looked at Lynton, and could say nothing.

"The body count is mounting," said the captain in a remorseful tone.

He stooped and looked again at the poor young seaman. He was very sombre as he said, "The poor devil. The poor devil was so young. What a shame."

One of the men grunted some of the huskiness out of his throat, and spoke. "Where we take him? The freezer is running out of space."

"Stack them if you must. Put him in quietly, as quietly as possible. This is a travesty."

Lynton, reflecting on all the noise and turmoil, looked about and wondered why not a single passenger had been aroused by all the commotion and come out on deck. It was nearly 8:00 AM and no one had come out of a cabin, not one passenger. Why? The passengers had been incognito almost the entire voyage, almost as if they were hiding from something, or were they waiting for something?

As they carried the poor young man and the others away, Lynton heard the morose, tired, discouraged captain make a deep guttural sound that was almost a groan. It was as if he had given up hope.

The rest of the men had gone about gathering bodies, and she did not think the captain realized that she was standing by his side. He shook his head, sighed deeply and said, "Oh my, oh my, what has been wrought? What? I say that once and for all time. What will make this end? What has been done to make us suffer this over again and again? How have we displeased God so much that he would put us through this hell? When will it end?"

Pinter departed without a word. He just looked at Lynton and shrugged his broad shoulders as if to say he was too perplexed for words. But there was more in his manner than that. It was as if he knew something, knew something very dark, sinister, foreboding that he was not sharing with her. She felt the need to find out what the captain meant by saying "make us suffer this again and again,"

 J. Wayne Frye

Chapter 9
More Questions in Her Furtive Mind

Humanity with all its fears,
With all the hopes of future years,
Is hanging breathless on Lynton's fate,
For her courage no one can abate.
The evil's breath she can feel,
But this woman is made of steel.

Who made each mast, and sail, and rope
For a ship with demons to cope.
What anvils rung, what hammers beat?
In what forge was eternity's heat?
Fear not each sudden sound and shock,
For Lynton is of wave and not of rock.

Is she the one who will never fail?
Does she not stand against the gale?
In spite of rock and tempest's roar,
In spite of false lights on the shore,
Does she refuse to cry frightened tears

Lynton & the Haunting
Of the HMS Wind Dancer

To stand triumphant over all fears?

The world unfortunately is not a place where good predominates, because if it did, the rich would not rule with the iron fist of economic oppression and injustice. If good triumphed more often, there would be no homeless people while the rich few live in palaces of excess. If evil did not permeate the core of men, no one would go hungry in a world where there is enough food for all. If evil did not lurk within the hearts of men, no child would die from lack of medical care while a vast amount of money was spent on weapons of war.

Evil predominates, because too many churches and mosques preach hate with finger-pointing as their de-facto creed. Religion is often not about acceptance, compassion and healing but about demonizing those who do not submit to the dictates of some magical king in the sky, dictates interpreted by a pack of self-righteous, arrogant, pompous, self-serving, bombastic, sanctimonious hypocrites. Thus is the modern world, where religion often does not unite but divides.

Evil seemed to always be triumphant. Lynton had seen it time and time again, and here on this ill-fated vessel, she saw evil taking form and wrecking havoc. Yet, there was an element she could not comprehend. There was something beneath the surface that was not evident, something that she was not able to grasp in her usual perceptive manner.

 J. Wayne Frye

Lynton & the Haunting
Of the HMS Wind Dancer

Despite her promise to her husband to give up demon hunting, it seemed that she was always putting herself in situations that brought him worry. It had been five days now, and, for some mysterious reason she had been unable to communicate with anyone on her cell phone. The crew, the captain, not one single passenger had displayed a cell phone. When she asked Pinter about the lack of coverage and why there was no WIFI, all he did was looked puzzled. She assumed that it was just the weird atmospheric conditions that seemed to be following the ship which prevented her from using a tool which the world had so enthusiastically embraced. Her husband called cell phones just another tool in corporations and governments march to create people who willingly lined up for their balls and chains. As cell phone service continued to increase in price, poor and affluent alike clung to them like they were precious commodities that were more valuable than gold. People could not see that they were being manipulated by corporations into a dependency that trapped them the rest of their lives and forced them to bow before their masters. She got a smile on her face as she thought of how her husband refused to have a cell phone, but still depended on a computer to write his books. He even refused to have television; having dumped it with his tirade that 250 channels of junk is still junk. That was her Wayne, a paradox if ever there was one. She got tears in her eyes, realizing how much she missed him.

Lynton & the Haunting
Of the HMS Wind Dancer

You were on my mind when I woke this morning.
Remembering your smile,
I guess the next time I'll see your face
Might take a little while.

I was remembering your arms around me
The way they always feel warm,
As having you right by my side
Makes me safe through any storm.

I was remembering your voice
That makes my heart skip a beat.
With you by my side
I am strong, never weak.

I was remembering our times
All the good and bad.
The times you cheered me up
When I was sad.

I was remembering your eyes,
And how they always meet mine,
Remembering all the things you do
To make everything so fine.

I was wondering when we'll be together
When it will be just us two.
I guess I'm just missing you
More than I usually do.

As she was reflecting on her love for Wayne, her concentration was broken with, "What's wrong?"

     J. Wayne Frye

She turned her head toward Pinter to reply to his question. "Nothing, just reflecting on how much I want this voyage to be over."

"You're not alone in that wish, Lynton. It seems like I have been on this voyage for a hundred years. It seems as if it will never end."

In a serious tone, she replied, "All things end, even pain. Unfortunately, the end is sometimes death. Of course, for those who are enduring great suffering, death can be a blessing. I am afraid the deaths on this ship are not a blessing, but then again, who am I to say, because I am lost in a mist of bewilderment over what is happening. I have faced many perils which my husband has chronicled in book after book, but I am not sure I have ever faced a peril like this one. This is a mystery that I seem unable to solve."

Pinter seemed lost in thought. He stood silent for awhile, and then said, "Maybe some things are not meant to be solved. Maybe things just happen for no apparent reason. I do not ascribe to the theory that things happen for a reason. Maybe it is because I am not religious."

"I am not religious either, as I have always seen the bad side of religion. The side that does not promote the ideals espoused by that man called Jesus. His messages of love, compassion, acceptance and forgiveness have been perverted by a church that is more interested in building monuments of excess and pointing the finger of condemnation than to extending a hand up to those crushed under the weight of greed and injustice."

"You are an exceptional woman, Lynton. I could see that from the first encounter with you, and I am not just talking about your physical beauty. You have an inner beauty that shines bright and warm like the midday sun."

Smiling, Lynton replied, "You are kind, but believe me, there is nothing that exceptional about me, and as for physical beauty, that fades with age, so without something besides that the beauty is always superficial."

"Don't sell yourself short lady."

Again smiling, she replied, "But I am short – only 5:2."

They shared a laugh, and Lynton knew that, like so many men, Pinter was enamoured with her. It was something she dealt with on a daily basis. Her husband had told her that she should enjoy the attention, because it represented who she was, and that it was not just her beauty and sensualness that attracted men, but her depth of character. There was an aura about her. She gave off an effervesce of character that elevated her onto a plain above the normal. She got tears in her eyes thinking about how much she was loved by her husband.

Pinter could tell she was in deep thought and said, "You're thinking about someone you love. Your husband I suppose."

"You are very perceptive. Yes, I am missing my husband, and counting the days, the hours, the minutes, the seconds until we will be together again.

"I wish I had someone to feel that way about."

Lynton & the Haunting
Of the HMS Wind Dancer

Feeling a tinge of pity for him, for anyone who needed love, she said, "You are a good man Harold. You will find that love one day."

"No, that time has passed for me. I am destined to sail the seas forever alone."

There was finality to his words; no, to his demeanour as he delivered them. He was carrying a heavy burden, and Lynton felt that she had to reach out to him and let him know she cared. Before she could get the words out that were forming in her brain, a seaman came running up and interrupted them.

He was frantic, as he blurted out, "Trouble sir! Trouble below. Come quickly."

Lynton fell in behind the two men as they raced below decks. What was wrong was not even shared, as they were in too big a hurry to talk.

It is a line from Coleridge's Ancient Mariner,
That reminded Lynton of what was to be.
By the staring, glistening of destiny's eye,
She wondered what evil they could see.

Hell's doors were opening wide,
And she felt like a next of kin;
The creatures will be met, the feast set:
She and the two, the vessel will defend.

The evil ones sat on a stone:
They could not speak but could hear;
And thus their evil was visual,
Which causes even more fear.

"What are we doing?" Lynton asked.

The seaman responded, "You'll see. Wait and see the evil. Just wait."

As they stepped into the hallway below the main deck, there was a shock when Lynton saw, for the first time, a passenger's cabin door ajar. The seaman put his right index finger to his lips and whispered, "Peep in, peep in."

Lynton and Pinter peered through the slightly opened door and there on the bed was a sight that sent chills up and down their spines. Two dark shadows were hovering over an obviously unconscious man and woman, and the shadows were sucking something out of the couple's bodies. A blue light-like substance was emanating from the mouths of the man and woman in a long, continuous stream. Despite the fright, Lynton and Pinter looked at one another with almost benign acceptance of what was going on, while the seaman stood behind them quietly.

Suddenly the bluish transparent light was all sucked up into the creatures. The couple was obviously dead, as the creatures of darkness, the shadows of hopelessness turned toward the three and the door, nearly knocking over Lynton and Pinter, slammed shut with a loud thud.

The three stood in shock as Pinter reached into his pocket and pulled out his pass key. He tepidly inserted it and opened the door. As he did, the two shadowy figures turned and whisked over them out the door, making the three duck for fear the shadows would engulf them.

　　　J. Wayne Frye

The three entered the room, closing the door behind them. Pinter and Lynton checked for a pulse on the bodies. There was none.

"How," asked Lynton of the seaman, "did you come upon this?"

"I was doing my duties and noticed the door slightly open. I peeped in and saw, saw what you just saw. Then, I just ran to find help."

The seaman was shivering with fear. Lynton touched his arm and said, "Don't worry. Whatever they are they have what they wanted. They will not be back in here."

"What, what is going on?" asked the seaman.

Pinter took a deep breath and replied, "I think you know. I think I know."

Lynton, surprised by his reply, was about to ask what he meant, when Pinter immediately told the sailor, "Go to the bridge and inform the captain what has happened, and bring some sailors back with you so we can take the bodies away. Be sure and bring two laundry bin baskets, so that we will be able to conceal the bodies."

"Aye, aye, sir."

As the sailor left for the bridge, Lynton was about to ask again about what Pinter had meant by his earlier statement to the sailor, when Pinter turned to her and said, "I don't understand how you got on this ship and how you got mixed up in all this?"

"My husband just wanted me to have a leisurely sea voyage for relaxation. I am to meet him in Lagos."

Lynton & the Haunting
Of the HMS Wind Dancer

"We never make it to Lagos," he said, making Lynton wonder why he used the past tense rather than the present tense. Then the surprised sailors came in with the laundry baskets and begin the gruesome task of removing the bodies.

After the sailors removed the bodies, Lynton watched Pinter close the cabin door. A male passenger at the end of the hallway opened his door, peered at the two and quickly closed it. They turned to leave and at the other end of the hallway, an elderly woman opened her door, looked at the two quizzically and than slammed her door shut. Lynton turned to Pinter and said, "Why is it that so few of the passengers ever stroll on the deck? I have only seen a few out and about, and only a handful ever in the main lounge?"

"They are cautious that is all."

"Cautious of what?"

"Maybe they are like you. Maybe they sense something is wrong with this ship."

"What makes you think I feel it is the ship, and not the creatures that is the problem?" asked Lynton.

"You are sometimes too smart for your own good, Lynton. You know things that no other mortals know. You sense things that no other mortals sense. You perceive the unperceivable. You dance to the beat of a different drummer. You are more than just a demon hunter. I had never heard of you until you came on this vessel, but it is easy to see that you are not just an ordinary woman. You are special."

     J. Wayne Frye

"Special? No, I am not special? I just have a sense of justice in a world where there is none for those of us who toil in obscurity for our daily bread. I see the world as it is, and it is not a very nice place for 99% of the inhabitants. I also see a world hidden from view, a world where demons wait to pounce on the unsuspecting, the easily fooled who fall for fairy tales that keep them imprisoned. The real demons are not just in the dark recesses of a place called hell, but rather the real hell is the lives people live every day, and the real demons are the greedy, self-absorbed people who prey upon them – the rich, the corporations, the governments with no compassion and no sense of justice."

Smiling with admiration, Pinter said, "Of course, of course. That is why you, I believe, think the problem is with the ship also. That it is not just the creatures, the dark shadows that are wrecking havoc on us all."

"I may be all wrong. It's only an idea of mine. I have no proof though, nothing concrete."

"What do you mean?"

"What I mean is I've nothing that the captain would consider as proof. He would never listen seriously to me."

"He'd listen now I am 100% sure. 100% I tell you. After what's happened down here in that cabin, he will absolutely listen to anything you have to say. Anyway, if you are the woman I think you are, you will tell him, and damn the repercussions."

"What could they do, anyway?" Lynton said, despondently. "As things are going, we'll all be dead before we reach Lagos, anyway."

"You tell what you have to say," he answered. "That's what you've got to do."

She shook her head and said, "You sure?"

"Well, anyway, he'll have to do something," he replied, in answer to her question. "We can't go on much longer with the number of crewmen we've lost. We haven't enough to handle the ship and the passengers."

"You don't understand," she said. "Even if I could get the captain to believe I've got at the truth of the matter, he couldn't do anything. Don't you understand? If what I think is true, we couldn't even see Lagos, if we made it there. We're like the blind. I think you know what I am getting at. I think you know this is about more than anyone wants to admit."

"What on earth do you mean?" he interrupted. "How do you make out we're like blind men? Of course we could see the land."

"Wait a minute!" she emphatically said. "You don't understand. Didn't I tell you?"

"Tell me what?" he asked.

"About the ship I spotted two days ago, she said. "Everyone should have seen it. It was off our starboard, maybe a few kilometres or so. Surely everyone saw it."

"No," he said. "No one saw anything."

"Are you sure? You mean there was no mention of a vessel starboard of us?"

"No, nobody saw nothing. If anybody had the knowledge of another ship it would have been shared with all." He then got a worried, quizzical look on his face.

Lynton said, "What is it? What are you thinking?"

There was momentary silence before Pinter replied. "You know what? I don't ever remember seeing ships, no ships no matter how many journeys I've made on this infernal ship. We never spot other ships. That's why we were so surprised by those lights."

Lynton, a look of surprise on her face, said, "So, you are telling me no one ever sees any other ships?"

"Right. Right. No one ever sees any ships. Ever!"

They walked up the stairs together, as Lynton said, "Then that confirms it."

"Confirms what?"

Taking a deep breath and exhaling slowly, Lynton replied, "There is a strange atmosphere, or whatever it is, as I alluded to earlier, that I believe we are in and it would not allow people to see another ship?"

"But you saw it. You saw a ship."

"That is what I cannot understand. Why I could see it. But then again, some of the crew did see the lights. And why, if we are only a few kilometres off the coast do we never see land? I don't have all the answers yet, but I am formulating the questions which may provide answers eventually."

"So, this strange atmospheric phenomenon you say is the cause of all of this?"

Shaking her head, Lynton replied, "For some of it, yes. You see for all intents and purposes we're blind. Just you think of it! We're out in the middle of the ocean, sort of playing blind man's bluff. You see, even if the captain wanted to put into port, he couldn't. He'd run us onto shore, without our ever seeing it. He'd wreck the ship on a dock or reefs or whatever."

"What of the creatures then? What of them?"

"They inhabit wherever we are, whatever dimension we have sailed into. They resent our intrusion and are attacking us for that reason."

"What are we going to do, then?" he asked, in a despairing sort of way. "Do you mean to say we can't do anything? Surely something can be done! There must be some way to get out of this predicament."

"That is the conundrum of a lifetime," offered Lynton.

They stood on deck, looking out into the fog, the thick fog that always seemed to shroud the ship. For perhaps a full minute, they paced up and down in the mist, until Pinter blurted out, "We might be run down, then," he said, "and never even see the other vessel?"

"It's possible," Lynton replied. "Though, from what I saw, it's evident that we're quite visible; so that it would be easy for them to see us, and steer clear of us, even though we couldn't see anything of them."

        J. Wayne Frye

"But we might run into something, and never see it?" he asked Lynton, following up the train of thought.

"Yes," she said. "Only there's nothing to stop the other ship from getting out of our way."

He made no reply and for a few moments they were quiet. Then he spoke abruptly, as though the idea had come suddenly to him. "Those lights the other night!" he said. "We saw them. At least most of us did. Were they a ship's lights?"

"I think so," Lynton replied. "Why?"

"Maybe there is an occasional hole, an opening of sorts in this atmospheric anomaly." He took a very deep breath and continued, "Won't do any good telling the captain this theory. He'll just laugh us off.

"I don't know," Lynton replied. "I've been thinking about it, and it can't do any harm. He already thinks I'm crazy anyway."

Pinter, with deep conviction said, "You needn't be afraid of anybody laughing at you. It might do some good. You've seen more than anyone else. You've experienced stuff like this before. You have a better perspective than most."

He looked up at the bridge and the faint outline the captain could be seen through the fog as he walked out the door onto the poop deck. "Come along now," Pinter said. "The skipper is up on the poop. No better time than right now."

She hesitated, but he caught her by the sleeve, and almost dragged her up the stairs to confront the captain. He greeted them with a scowl.

The first mate was alongside the captain and he dismissed him with the order, "Bring him here."

Before the mate could leave, Lynton, said, "I think you should stay. I need to speak to you and the captain."

The captain nodded to the mate, indicating he should stay. He said to Lynton, "Get on with it woman. What is it?"

Lynton, never at a loss for words, somehow had trouble getting what she was thinking to convert to the verbal. "I scarcely know how to put this, captain." Then she remembered that she had never heard the captain's name mentioned, and interrupted her train of thought by saying, "I don't know your name, sir. All I know is captain, captain what?"

Then, he very dismissively said, "Just captain will do."

Not wanting to cause any more animosity, Lynton let it pass and said, "I scarcely know how to put it, sir. It's - it's about these - these things."

"What things? Speak out, woman." he said.

"Well, sir," she blurted out. "The things we have all seen, these entities that come aboard the ship."

He gave a quick look to the first mate and then replied. "How do you mean come aboard?"

"Out of the sea, sir," she said. "I've seen them. We've all seen them."

"Ah!" he exclaimed, and it seemed to her, from his facial expression, that he understood where this was leading. He repeated, "Out of the sea, you say?"

"Yes sir," she said. "It's the ship. I've watched. I've observed closely. I think I understand a bit; but there's a lot I still don't comprehend."

Sighing, the captain said, "OK, I'll grant you that I am not a master at understanding the supernatural. However, I have had many voyages on this ship, many voyages trying to get things right, and I will eventually get it right, get everything just perfect. Little lady, you don't know half as much as you think you know." Then he looked over at Pinter and continued, "This man, like many others on this ship is painfully unaware at times of just how each voyage on this ship has to be completed to perfection. A set of rules are in place and must be followed. We do not control our destinies. I don't know how you got on this ship, but, believe me, it was a mistake of monumental proportions. You are not supposed to be here."

She was confused by the statement, but let it slide, because she did not want to get off the subject at hand. She said, "We both know captain that something is determined to wreck havoc on this ship, something that is coming up out of the sea to seek out the living and destroy them."

"You've seen things come out of the sea, you say? All I have seen are shadows. Never saw anything come out of the sea. Now just tell me all you can remember, from the very beginning. Tell me each little thing that will enlighten me. Open up the treasure chest of information that is going to elevate my intelligence so that I might successfully confront the terror on this ship."

She told him everything in detail, commencing with the strange man who had sat beside her that very first day and then about the figure that had stepped aboard out of the sea, and continuing her yarn, up to the things that had happened before the captain's eyes. She stuck well to solid facts; and now and then the captain and the mate would look at one another and nod. At the end, he turned to her with an abrupt gesture.

"You still hold, then, that you saw a ship. A ship no one else on watch saw?

"Yes, sir," she said. "I most certainly do. There was a ship; and, if you will let me, I believe that I can explain its presence."

"Well," he gruffly replied. "Go on."

Now that she knew he was willing to listen to her in a serious manner, she brazenly shared every single item with him. She ended by saying, "It was suggested we put into port, but I do not think we can, as I alluded to earlier in my explanation. There are things that people on this ship cannot see. As I said, all are blind in a strange sort of way."

"But you are not, of course," interrupted the captain.

"For some reason, yes," answered Lynton. "Yes, I can see things the rest of you apparently can't. I have no explanation for it, but I think that is pretty evident."

"You could be right. Yes, it could be that the rest of us, for a reason that is just lying there on the surface waiting to be discovered, can't."

Lynton & the Haunting
Of the HMS Wind Dancer

Lynton got a quizzical look on her face, as the captain continued. "So, you don't think we can see land, uh? Even if it is there, we can't see it?"

"Well, sir," she replied. "If we're unable to see other vessels, we shouldn't be able to see the land. You'd be piling the ship up, without ever seeing where you were putting her."

"But you can see other vessels, so you should be able to see the land; consequently, I could let you be our eyes, could I not?"

"Maybe, sir. Maybe I could."

"Can you explain why the men saw those lights? I mean you say we are blind to other vessels and land. Why did they see the lights?"

"All I know is I believe we have sailed into another plain of existence by accident, and that is why we are being attacked. Those things, whatever they are, resent out intrusion, resent us being here, but maybe the men saw those lights, because somehow there was a brief opening, a window if you will, into the real world, the plain we are supposed to be in."

In that place, at that time, a bright beacon of hope was lit by an incredible woman who knew the meaning of compassion. All there gazed at her with admiration.

Looking over at the helmsman, then back at Lynton, the captain said, "We are going to make it to Lagos this trip. We are going to make it. You little lady are our salvation, our hope to end a nightmare that has plagued this vessel far too long."

Lynton could not figure out what he meant by "this trip" and "this time." Some things were clearer, and still other things had created even more questions in her furtive mind.

 J. Wayne Frye

Chapter 10
Will There Be a Tomorrow?

Humanity with all its fears,
With all the hopes of future years,
Is hanging breathless on Lynton's fate,
For her courage no one can abate.

The evil's breath she can feel,
But this woman is made of steel.
She commands eternal hope
For a ship with demons to cope?

What anvils ring, what hammers beat?
In what forge is eternity's heat?
No ghost can arise in her fright,
For she carries good's light.

Fear not each sudden sound and shock,
For Lynton is of wave and not of rock.
Is it she the one who will never fail?
Does she not stand against the gale?

Lynton & the Haunting
Of the HMS Wind Dancer

In spite of rock and tempest's roar,
In spite of false lights on the shore,
She refuses to cry frightened tears,
Standing triumphant over all fears?

Lynton lay on her bed, staring at the ceiling. Her eyes were wide open, but she was asleep. She began to see a vision take place on the ceiling. A man's face came into view. His eyes were extraordinarily piercing and passionate, with the deep brilliance in them such as may be noticed in the insane. The lower part of his face was hidden in hair, but the skin, as much of it as was visible, for his cap was dragged low down upon his brows, was pale, of a haggard shallowness, expressed best in paintings of the dead where time has produced the fading of the pigment. Yet, his graveyard complexion did not detract from the majesty and imperiousness of his mien and port. She could readily conceive that the defiance of his heart would be hell-like in obstinacy, and that here was a man whose pride and passions would qualify him for a foremost place among the most daring of those fallen spirits of whom glorious poets had written. Was he evil or was he good? Was he dead or was he alive?

She sprang up instantly, awakening with a revelation of what she heard the two sailors whispering about. She reflected on when she heard them mention *the Dutchman*, because as she reflected on all that had occurred, it suddenly came to her what they were perhaps referring to in

     J. Wayne Frye

their hushed whispers. She remembered the tale, a tale of a derelict ship that was supposed to have sailed the seas for hundreds of years.

Yes, she had heard her husband talk of the *Flying Dutchman* once as he was working on one of his books. It was a ship that can never make port and is doomed to sail the oceans forever. Sightings in the 18th, 19th and 20th centuries reported the ship to be glowing with a ghostly light. If hailed by another ship, the crew of the *Flying Dutchman* will appear as undulating ghosts. In ocean lore, the sight of this phantom ship is a portent of doom for whomever and whatever vessel comes across it.

Lynton had seen it that night. She had seen it astern, bearing down on the Wind Dancer. That sailing ship was not from the 1800's. It was from the 1700's, and it was the *Flying Dutchman*. Lynton had seen it, and when it is seen there is doom waiting. How could she save the Wind Dancer and its crew? How could she save herself? Were those shadows ghosts mere scouts from the *Flying Dutchman*, which was trailing them, had been trailing them for days?

She contemplated telling the captain again what she had seen, a ship that portended doom for them all, but what difference would that make? How could that alter the events as they were currently perceived? It would make no difference, as their only hope was for the captain to make her their eyes, so that he could bring the ship safely into Lagos Harbour.

Lynton & the Haunting
Of the HMS Wind Dancer

She left her cabin to stroll above in the crisp air of the sea night. Although the ship was shrouded in mist and the usual fog, the sea was mostly calm with the ship lifting ever so slightly to an occasional glassy heave. The only sounds that struck on the ear were the soft, slow rustle and occasional shiver of a slight breeze, and the continuous and monotonous creak, creak of the gentle movements of the vessel.

She came upon Pinter and smiled. He smiled back, but the smile suddenly became a scowl as he pointed to the stern of the ship. He whispered, "Look."

She looked backward, but saw nothing. She said, "What?"

"That queer shadow, that big, very big shadow that seems to be following us."

And then she saw exactly what he meant. It was something big and shadowy that appeared to be growing clearer, morphing from transparency into more solid form.

"Look at it!" said Pinter, again. "It is growing in size."

As they peered down at it, the thing seemed to be rising up and down, floating as it were, like a ship riding the waves. It was taking shape. Lynton knew exactly what it was as she said, "See, it is like the shadow of a ship."

And it was. It was the distinguishable shadow of a ship rising out of the unexplored immensity behind the Wind Dancer's stern.

"What's this mean? asked Pinter.

             J. Wayne Frye

Lynton & the Haunting
Of the HMS Wind Dancer

"It, my dear Pinter, is what so many of you on board have suspected all along, I think. I believe you have all been afraid to admit the truth, to admit that this vessel is being shadowed by the famous *Flying Dutchman* ghost ship. I saw the ship before one night, saw it in the darkness trailing us, and my guess is that those lights we have been seeing are not beacons, but lamps from the 1700's burning whale oil. You are able to see that. We are all able to see that. We are not blind to some things – to ghost ships we are not blind. We can all see that ship. You see it now. You see the *Flying Dutchman*.

Looking with immense admiration at Lynton, Pinter said, "And you know where the *Flying Dutchman* was sunk hundreds of years ago?"

"Cape of Good Hope, right near Cape Town Harbour," replied a confident Lynton. Then she went on. "And, my guess is that since we left Cape Town Harbour, we have been followed by the *Dutchman*. Many of the crew think the same. I am sure."

"And now, you assume that the entities, the shadows, are ghostly scouts from that ship. But why the murders of the crew? Why would the ghosts, the shadows want to take lives?"

"That one I am still working on," replied Lynton.

The first mate and the captain came up, and could tell something was up. The captain, with a gruff manner, said, "When you two are together, it is not usually good news."

Pinter turned toward the stern and pointed. "Right below the railing you can see it, see a sailing vessel with full masts."

For a little while, the captain and the first mate just stared intensely, as did Lynton and Pinter. Then the captain and the first mate looked at one another and said, "Don't see nothing. Do you?"

Bewildered, Lynton and Pinter both in unison said, "It was there."

The captain, to Lynton's surprised, did not scoff at her, but simply asked, "Explain?"

Pinter did not hesitate to say, "Tell him Lynton, tell him the whole story just as you told me."

Lynton explained to the captain her theory, and her astonishment continued, because, again, he did not question her veracity. Rather, he looked to be deep in thought, considering all she had shared.

The captain looked her in the eyes and said, "So, you saw a shadow of what you assume is a ship, a ship that you have seen before, a ship that you say has been following us since we left Cape Town, and your deduction is that it is the *Flying Dutchman* of legend?"

"That sir is indeed my deduction."

"And you Pinter. You saw this thing, too?"

"I did sir, and it was obviously a vessel, an old sailing vessel at full mast. It was not our imaginations."

Looking intently at Pinter, the captain said, "Perhaps we should tell her all we know, every last thing in regards to what is going on. She may well be able to handle the truth."

Pinter replied, "Do we really know sir, or only suspect?"

Lynton, almost pleading said, "Please, I have a right to know."

"Maybe you do," replied the captain, but then he took a deep breath and sighed as he continued, "but now is not the time. Not until we are 100% sure that is the *Flying Dutchman* somehow pursuing us."

"What are you hiding," pleaded Lynton.

"In due time, in due time," replied the captain.

Lynton looked at Pinter with pleading eyes. He said, "Not now Lynton. Now is simply not the time."

"There are ten people dead. How many more must die before it will be time?"

The captain, eyes seeming to tear up, said, "If you only knew how many have died. My, woman, you have no idea. Be patient and all will be clear eventually, but when it is, it may be too late for all of us, including you. You should have never been on this ship. Your being here is a mistake that may well cost you your life."

The three men turned and walked away, leaving Lynton to contemplate what they meant. She thought a lot about the shadow vessel. And then she got another thought; for she got thinking of the figures she had seen aloft in the early morning; and she began to imagine fresh things. You see, that first thing that had come up over the side had come out of the sea, or had it come from that vessel that was trailing the Wind Dancer? And were those shadows, those evil entities from the ghost ship? There was one entity that she was not sure of, that old man who had sat beside her on the deck. He had warned her, and never made any move to harm her or anyone else.

Pinter returned, and immediately admonished her not to ask what he and the captain knew that they were not ready to share. She said, "OK," and then told him that she was convinced those shadows were from the ghost ship trailing them. He accepted that theory without reservation.

"Why," asked Pinter, "do those things take lives?"

"There is a bluish light comes out of people. No, it is sucked out of people. Those things are somehow feeding on the living, taking some essence from their bodies."

Pinter looked puzzled, as he said, "Could they take it from the dead, also?"

"What do you mean?"

"Well, suppose someone was dead, could they get that essence from a dead person?"

Lynton thought awhile, and then replied. "Maybe, it is possible I suppose."

Pinter seemed in deep thought for awhile, and Lynton wondered what he was thinking, but before she could ask, he blurted out. "Is it possible other ghost ships are out here?"

"I think it possible, even probable. If we could alter course I believe we might somehow break away from these entities, the ghost ship, but the captain will not alter the course."

          J. Wayne Frye

"That cannot happen, Lynton."

"Why? She asked.

Smiling, he said, "You know I am not at liberty to tell you that yet. Just accept the fact that our course will not, cannot be altered."

The first mate suddenly yelled over at the two from the aft railing, "Pinter, over here, quick."

He looked over at Lynton and shrugged his shoulders. The mate yelled, "OK, bring the little miss buttinski, too. But for goodness sake, hurry. Hurry, I tell ya."

They got there and he was leaning over the railing, looking aft into the water. "Look!" he said, and pointed right directly behind them.

The water was momentarily blurred, so that Lynton and Pinter could not see. Then, as the ripples cleared away, they saw what he meant. "Two of them!" he said, in a voice that was scarcely above a whisper. "And there's another out there," he continued as he pointed again.

Looking intently, Lynton muttered, "And there is another a little further aft."

"Where? Where?" the mate asked.

"There," she said as she pointed at the dark shadow that was undulating just above the water line.

"Damnable shadows," offered the mate. "There's four of the things."

Lynton and Pinter said nothing, just stared into the ocean. The shadows appeared to be out to sea, maybe a good 200 metres away, perhaps more. They were suddenly quite motionless.

Yet, although their outlines were somewhat blurred and indistinct, there was no mistaking they were the same creatures. Then, far out behind the shadows came another figure, one even more menacing looking and much bigger. It was a full mast flowing in the breeze old-time sailing vessel. Slowly it came out of the fog, becoming clearer and clearer. Before, it had never been really clear, but this time there was no mistaking what it was. How bold, how utterly awe-inspiring, even though it appeared menacing. It was a rare old craft, a true ship of the old school, no doubt large for its time. It had a claw-footed, full-breasted, half-woman half-creature on the bow, seeming to cut through the night air like a knife slicing through warm butter with ease of purpose. Long seasoned and weather-stained in the typhoons and storms of a churning ocean, her old hull was darkened with all the years of the lonely search for an end to plying the sea forever and ever, and it had the complexion of a woman who had fallen victim to time, but not given into the process of ageing deep inside. You could sense that within this ship were ghosts who were as bold, free and determined as anything that had ever plied the seven seas. The masts with full dirtied white sails stood stiffly like the spines of warriors who would not yield before sword, shot or shell. This was a presence that instilled fear, yes, but oh, how it also inspired awe.

The mate shouted, "Gotta tell the captain."

Pinter pointed up to the bridge, where everyone was peering out aft and said, "Don't need to."

Lynton & the Haunting
Of the HMS Wind Dancer

For some minutes those on the bridge, those on watch and Pinter, the mate and Lynton watched in awe, without speaking. At last Pinter spoke. "They're real, right enough," he said. "They and the ship are definitely real."

Lynton, ever the philosophical sage, said, "Real? Maybe, maybe not. One man's reality is another man's fiction."

"What do you mean?"

"Well, my husband often says, 'one man's terrorist is another man's freedom fighter.' So, I would say it all depends on your perspective."

Before long, the captain was alongside the three, peering aft. He said to Lynton, "My goodness."

"Indeed," replied Lynton.

After that, for some half-minute, they all stared, without a word. The captain struck Lynton as looking, in an unusual sense, not worried, as if he had somehow seen all this before. She wondered if he had, indeed, come across the phantom ship and the creatures before.

"What's your inclination," said Lynton, interrupting the silence.

"To sail this vessel as I always sail her."

Surprised at his lack of concern, Lynton said, "You are not serious?"

"As serious as anyone can get," replied the captain, as he turned and walked away, motioning for Pinter to follow.

The mate stood for awhile and could not form any words, nor could Lynton. They were both mystified by the captain's lack of concern.

Lynton & the Haunting
Of the HMS Wind Dancer

Looking aft, the two saw a heavy fog close in and the shadows and the ghost ship disappeared in the mist, as if they had never even been there. The mate shrugged his shoulders and walked away.

Lynton stood watching the sun set through dark clouds and noticed something that otherwise she should, most probably, under quiet normal circumstances, have missed. The sun had dipped nearly half-way below the horizon, and was showing like a great, red dome of dull fire. Abruptly, far away on the starboard bow, a faint mist drove up out of the sea. It spread across the face of the sun, so that its light shone as though it came through a dim haze of smoke. Quickly, this mist or haze grew thicker; but, at the same time, separating and taking strange shapes, so that the red of the sun struck through ruddily between them. Then, as she watched, the weird mistiness collected and shaped and rose into three towers. These became more definite, and there was something elongated beneath them. The shaping and forming continued, and almost suddenly she saw that the thing had taken on the shape of that infernal trailing ship. Directly afterwards, she saw that it was moving. It had been broadside on to the sun. Now it was swinging. The bow came round with a stately movement, until the five masts bore in a line. It was heading directly towards the Wind Dancer. It grew larger; but yet less distinct. Astern of it, she saw now that the sun had sunk to a mere line of light. Then, in the gathering dusk it seemed to her that the ship was sinking back into the

          J. Wayne Frye

ocean. The sun went beneath the sea, and the thing she had seen became merged, as it were, into the lonely darkness of the coming night.

The night had come down strangely dark. Yet, the dark and the stillness, the rolling, the rising and lowering of the ship made Lynton only conscious in occasional flashes of comprehension. For, now that her mind was working in slow tandem with the motion of the ship, she was thinking chiefly of that queer, vast phantom of mist she had seen rise from the sea, and take shape. She kept staring into the night towards the vastness of an incomprehensible darkness that seemed to be calling all aboard to join the ghosts of a ship that was stuck sailing for all eternity. She felt a cold shiver throughout her body and had a horrible feeling that something beastly was going to happen any minute.

Yet, time, like the vessel upon which she stood, marched inexorably on, and still all was quiet, strangely quiet. No disaster was materializing. Still, she shivered in dread. And there were, as always, no passengers about. Why? Why did they seem reluctant to venture from their cabins, save the few who could be seen in the main lounge area on occasion?

Three times already she had seen the watch-seaman down onto the main deck, prowling about like a cat on a hot tin roof. She guessed that he had been sent to look out at the distant sea for any signs of that abominable ship that might not be visible from the bridge.

Lynton & the Haunting
Of the HMS Wind Dancer

Oh, how astutely alert was the dynamic dynamo when anticipation of trouble was being pondered within her ever furtive mind. There was something unaccountably strange in the air that night. How does one account for the hair raising on the back of the neck, the tingling sensation within the chest, the rapid flow of blood to the brain and the sudden rapid breathing? Is it a way for the body to warn us to prepare for danger?

In an instant, she heard an unintelligible shout from above, then something whizzing through the air and a loud thud when something hit the deck near the bow. From the main deck there came the sound of running feet, and the voices of seaman, shouting. Then she caught the captain's voice. He must have run out on deck through the main lounge doorway.

"Get some lights over here," he shouted, as Lynton ran toward the bow, but was stopped by a lifeboat that had fallen from above and, lying on its crumbled side, was preventing her from getting to where the captain and some crewmen had congregated.

She caught only two words from the captain, "carried away."

Then she heard a seaman say, "No sir, don't think so."

She listened intently, but did not venture any farther. A minute of some confusion followed; and then came the click of and clang of men scurrying about. She heard the captain, but could not make out what he was saying. He was asking a question.

     J. Wayne Frye

She did hear one of the seaman say, "Can't say, sir." He continued after a slight pause, "Seems alright."

She did not hear the captain's reply; for in the same moment, there came to her a chill of cold breath at her back. She turned sharply, and saw something standing maybe ten feet aft from her. The thing stood on the outside of the railing, just stood in thin air as if there were a floor under it. It had eyes that reflected a deep longing, weirdly, with a frightful, intense gleam; but beyond that, she could see nothing with any distinctness. For the moment, she just stared. She seemed frozen. It was so close. Then, movement came to her finally willing body, and she jumped to her left behind the stairs to the upper deck.

The thing, whatever it was, had come more forward over the rail; but now, before the light, it recoiled with a queer, horrible litheness as Lynton shouted, "Away, away you devil!"

It slid back, and down, and out of sight as the captain, with Pinter and three other men, having heard Lynton's admonition to the creature, managed to crawl over the fallen lifeboat and rush to her side.

"What the devil's up now?" shouted the captain as Pinter reached out and pulled Lynton up off the deck floor under the stairs.

She stood up and tried to answer with calmness. "Saw one of them. It was breathing down my neck. I assume something has thrown the lifeboat down from the upper deck."

"Correct little lady," replied the captain.

Lynton, calm and direct, said, "I wish I knew what you were hiding from me. It might make it easier to solve this mystery."

The captain took a deep breath and said, "My dear, this is all old hat to me and the boys here. Sometimes our minds draw a blank, and a few times, like right now, we can remember things we'd rather forget. Our memories come and go, you see. <u>If you knew the real truth, you'd likely jump overboard. I don't know how it happened, but I tell you that somehow you wound up where you weren't supposed to be. You are in a pickle, and frankly, I don't know how to get you out of it.</u>"

Behind the captain stood Pinter and he put his right index finger to his lips as if to indicate that Lynton should keep her mouth shut and not press the matter. She felt that he might be saying, "I'll tell you later what is going on."

"Tell me later," she thought? This whole affair reminded her of what Wayne sometimes said, "Think things are bad now? Wait until tomorrow."

She whispered to herself, "Will there be a tomorrow?"

Chapter 11
She Shed Tears for Him

*The evil some greeted with out-stretched hands.
Swiftly did creatures from below come atop,
Up from below in darkness,
With evil that would not stop.*

*The malicious ones came up upon the left;
Out of the sea creatures came to be.
And they were dark not bright, and on the right
They disappeared down again into the sea.*

When next Lynton saw Pinter, as she stood by the railing and prepared to ask him to explain what the captain was hiding and what he had meant by his most recent words to her about knowing the real truth, before she got any words out, a seaman came running up to him shouting, "Thorn is gone, clean vanished! I never was in such a damned, hair-raisin' experience before. It ain't safe on this here ship. Even dead people ain't safe."

Hearing those last words raised those proverbial hairs on the back of Lynton's neck. She thought about the ten who were dead. Were those creatures going to go after them, too? Was the sailor right? Were dead people not even safe?

"You saying that Thorn, the apprentice has disappeared?" asked Pinter.

"Yep, we been huntin' for quarter an hour now. Nowhere in sight he is, nowhere. We're still at it, but we'll never find him alive," he concluded, with a sort of gloomy assurance.

"Oh, I wouldn't be so sure," said Pinter. "Perhaps he slipped off somewhere for a nap, and he just hasn't woke up yet."

"Not him," replied the sailor. "I tell you we've turned everythin' upside down. He's not aboard the bloomin' ship."

"Where was he when they last saw him? Lynton asked. "Someone must know something."

"Keepin' time up on the poop," he replied. "The skipper's nearly shook the life out of everybody. And they say they don't know nothin'. Yet, the skipper said something really odd. He said that this is what we should expect. That we should be used to it by now. And you know what, that kind of rings true for some funny reason, but I just can't figure out why. Been tryin' to figure it out."

"How do you mean?" Lynton inquired as she glanced out of the side of her eye over at Pinter who seemed annoyed at the seaman. "Well," he answered as Pinter gave him a glare, "we all had our backs to him. We turned and he was gone."

     J. Wayne Frye

"Best let it go and get busy looking," interjected Pinter.

Lynton said, "Wait a minute. Answer me one more question."

Before she could finish, Pinter interrupted. "On with you job sailor. On with your duty."

Fearful of displeasing a superior officer, he did not wait for Lynton's question. He scurried away.

Lynton, perturbed at Pinter, said, "What is it you don't want him to tell me?"

"Nothing. He just has his duty to do. That's all."

"Is it?" she said.

"No need to get huffy about it. It's his job to look for the missing sailor, not stand around and idly gossip."

"Sometimes gossiping is beneficial. Sometimes, the truth can come out in that idol gossip you are so all fired worried about."

"I am telling you Lynton that you are getting in too deep. I am trying to protect you, trying to make sure you get off this ship alive."

Lynton wanted to open her mouth to tell him the probability was that she and none of them were going to make it off that vessel alive, even if they could get the captain to alter course. She looked at him with pleading eyes and said, "You all know this ship is haunted, not just by those creatures, but by a malevolence that has been about for many, many years. That man I have seen is a ghost that cannot free himself from this ship. He has been trying to warn me from the very beginning. He has the power of speech sometimes."

"I know who that creature is," offered Pinter.

"What? You know, you know who it is?"

"I do, yes."

"Please, I need to know."

"In 1968, this ship made an ill-fated voyage, and one of the passengers, a stowaway, claimed to be seeing a ghost ship, a sailing vessel that was trailing the Wind Dancer. No one believed him. Everyone thought he was crazy, as he did act deranged. They locked him below decks in a storage closet in the forward hold. He was forgotten, left there for six days with no food or water. They remembered after six days, but when they found him, he had died of dehydration. He left a note, scrawled in the dust on the floor. It said, "This ship will forever be doomed, and the Dutchman shall one day destroy it."

Lynton knew then that the old man that sat beside her was the ghost of the individual who died from lack of water. She shook her head and said, "No one is safe then?"

"Lynton, all I want is to get you safely off this ship. As we near Lagos, I will put you adrift in a lifeboat and you can escape this terror. I'll give you a compass and show you how to follow it to Lagos Harbour. The rest of us, I am afraid, are doomed."

"You are saying I should leave while the other passengers are left aboard to meet a fate foretold by a deranged man, a fate that will render them victims of a ghost ship, a ghost ship that has been trailing us since we left Cape Town?"

          J. Wayne Frye

"Lynton, all these passengers have been doomed from the start, doomed to face a fate that has awaited them for years and years. I cannot explain it; only tell you that what is going to happen has happened many times before."

That makes no sense, no sense at all," replied an exasperated Lynton.

With a note of finality in his voice, Pinter said, "It defies explanation, but all of us on-board suffer from delusions, delusions that make us think we can beat this thing, beat this evil, but we cannot."

Never one to give up, Lynton said, "What's going to be the end of it all then? Surely something can be done?"

Pinter said nothing. He just shrugged his shoulders and looked like a man without hope. He had come to the end of his rope it appeared. He had accepted the fate that had followed him in the form of a ship transporting evil.

"Surely, there is something can be done? Anything at all is better than just waiting, waiting for death."

Still, he said nothing; but stared moodily down into the water. She was pleading now. "You cannot give up! Do you hear me?"

"Yes, but you do not understand. You don't know the whole story."

"Then tell me the whole story. Make me understand why you had rather give up than fight? What is it that makes all of you seem so unwilling to fight? Why cannot any of you muster the courage to stand against this evil?"

Lynton & the Haunting
Of the HMS Wind Dancer

"We are exhausted," offered Pinter. "We've done all we can and it never does any good. We, like the *Dutchman*, are destined to sail these seas forever. I don't know what else we can do, unless we go below and lock ourselves in every night, lock ourselves away from the evil."

In an exasperated tone, Lynton said, "That would be better than this. Why don't the men do something? They ought to make the captain put us into port! I have already agreed to be his eyes."

"For goodness sake Lynton, shut up," Pinter uncharacteristically said. "What's the good of talking a lot of ridiculous rot like that? It's been tried before don't you see?"

With that, Lynton glanced over into the sea aft. The action had been almost mechanical; yet, after a few seconds, she was in a state of the most intense excitement, and without withdrawing her gaze, she reached out and caught Pinter's arm to attract his attention.

She muttered, as she pointed aft. "Look, look, I tell you."

"What is it?" he asked, and bent over the rail, beside her to look back where she was pointing. What they saw seared their minds with fright. A little distance behind, skimming the surface there lay that mighty sailing ship, that dark and evil looking five mast terror that was as relentless as an American Republican politician demanding tax cuts for the rich. It seemed only a few hundred feet behind them. On it, they saw quite clearly, after a few moments' staring, the shadows of

     J. Wayne Frye

obvious seamen with darkened hands held high in front of them as if they were going to propel themselves up and outward over the ocean.

"My goodness," belted out Pinter. "My goodness, she means business. She means to board us. It is early this time."

The huge, shadowy masts were not just bellowing without any breeze. They seemed to be almost lifting the ship into flight, and there was no mist, no fog, no darkness this time. This was a ship heading for a rendezvous of murderous intent, a bellowing, belching with evil malevolent force bent on destruction. You could actually feel the evil emanating from the decks where the shadowy figures were now completely morphing into men holding bright sabres that were glistening in the arriving moonlight.

There was movement on the deck of the *Dutchman*, coordinated movement that meant terror was about to rain down upon the Wind Dancer like lava from an exploding volcano roaring down the side of a mountain top that had just exploded with a fury.

Lynton glanced up at the bridge, and all there were in obvious terror, for they had seen what was coming their way. Upon their faces was recognition of the hopelessness of their situation. Recognition that the doors of hell had been opened and the demons of darkness were about to be let loose to bring carnage upon the crew and passengers of the Wind Dancer. The end was at hand.

Lynton looked into the eyes of Pinter, and she saw in them a depth of love for her that touched her soul. This man truly loved that which was unattainable. She shed tears for him.

     J. Wayne Frye

Lynton & the Haunting
Of the HMS Wind Dancer

Chapter 12
Welcome Aboard Little Lady

See you beneath the cloud so dark,
Fast gliding along, a gloomy bark?
Her sails are full, though the wind is still,
And there blows not a breath her sails to fill!

Oh! What doth that vessel of darkness bear?
The silent calm of the grave is there,
Save now and again a death-knell rung,
And the flap of the sails, with night-fog hung!

There lies a wreck on the dismal shore
Of cold and pitiless, evil gore,
Where, under the moon, upon mounts of frost,
Full many a mariner's bones are lost!

Yonder shadowy bark hath been to that wreck,
And the dim blue fire that lights her deck
Doth play on as pale and livid a crew
As ever yet drank the devil's brew!

Lynton & the Haunting
Of the HMS Wind Dancer

To Dead-Man's Isle, in the eye of the blast,
To Dead-Man's Isle, she speeds very fast;
By skeleton shapes her sails are furled,
And the hand that steers is not of this world!

Oh! Hurry thee on. Oh! Hurry thee on,
Thou terrible bark! Where the night be gone,
And the morn will look on so foul a sight,
As the Flying Dutchman dims hope's light.

Lynton could actually see those manifestations with sabres in clinched hands moving and glinting faintly and rapidly to and fro on the deck as the *Dutchman* closed in. There were glints in their eyes for they were relishing the taste of battle, the taste of blood, the taste of that blue essence.

Unconsciously, she must have leant farther and farther out over the side, staring; and suddenly how she yelled as she over balanced and made a sweeping grab, and caught the fore brace, and with that was able to keep from tumbling overboard. In the same second, she saw the passengers who never came out pouring from every door onto the deck, not in fighting mood, but seemingly lining up to await the taste of sabres that were about to slice them up. It was as if they had been waiting all this time for the *Dutchman's* crew, waiting to taste their fates. They were not alarmed. They were not afraid. They simply were there embracing their fate. This was about to be a blood bath, as Lynton looked to the aft and saw grappling ropes tossed over the railing, hooking an

     J. Wayne Frye

iron grappler to the rails, and then men began climbing aboard, preparing with glee for the assault.

They ran the passengers through with their blades, gutting them like poor cattle in a slaughter pen. As the passengers precipitously fell, the slayer would bend over them and from the dead passengers' mouths they would suck out some blue light, then move on to the next passenger. Why, she wondered, were none of the passengers bleeding from the wounds?

Above, on the bridge, the captain and those around him simply observed the carnage without any obvious passion. Finally, they walked slowly out onto the deck to meet their fates. It was getting darker; but that did not hide from Lynton a terrible and extraordinary sight. All along the port rail there was a queer, undulating greyness that moved downwards onboard, and spread over the decks, like a blanket of terror. As she observed all the rampaging one hundred strange men with swords ramming through bodies and then sucking that blue mist from the dead, in the half-light, they appeared unreal and impossible, as though there had come upon them, the inhabitants of some fantastic dream-world on a ship called the Wind Dancer. She thought, for a second, that she was mad. They swarmed in upon them in a great wave of murderous, living shadows of seafarers from the 1700's.

Not from a single passenger or crew member had a word been uttered, nor were there any screams. It was as if they were simply expecting this carnage and rather than fighting it, they embraced it with calm resignation.

She could not imagine why she and Pinter had not been gutted yet, for they stood there in the open. As she looked on, despite the darkness, she found that she saw more clearly, in a most extraordinary way, why she and Pinter were being spared. There, between them and the marauding hordes stood that old man who had sat by her side in what seemed now, an eternity ago. He stood like a bulwark of protection, as the marauders seemed unwilling to penetrate the area behind him where Lynton and Pinter stood.

That dark figure of a man turned and looked at Lynton. Then he looked at Pinter. Then he looked over at a donut life buoy hanging on the bulwark. He nodded at Pinter.

Pinter quickly walked over and took it down, returning to Lynton in a flash. He forced it around her thin body, bringing it to a halt around her tiny waist. She tried to keep him from doing it, but he was much stronger than she was. As she realized what he was about to do, she was pleading with her eyes for him to come with her. He said, "I cannot come. I must meet my destiny once again. I love you Lynton Viñas."

She tried to fight him, but it was to no avail as he lifted her up and tossed her over the railing. All at once, it seemed to her that it was darker than it had been the previous moment, and she raised her head, very cautiously. She looked up from the dark water and saw that the ship was enveloped in great billows of mist, and she could no longer see the carnage, only the occasional blue mist that was obviously being sucked from the dead bodies by the boarders from the *Flying Dutchman*. Finally, the ship simply disappeared from view as she drifted out to sea.

She actually did not feel safer now that she was bobbing about in the dark water hidden by the fog. She glanced around, and wondered if this fate might be worse than that she would have suffered had she stayed aboard, as she was all alone in a vast ocean. She felt a little cowardly that she was obviously the only survivor.

Her eyes glanced level with the distant dark horizon illuminated by the exceedingly bright full moon that was now hanging in the sky. The brightness danced upon the waves that swept toward her as she bobbed up and down. The waves were grey, except for the tops, which were white. The line between sky and water narrowed and widened, fell and rose.

A particular danger of the open sea is the fact that after successfully getting through one wave, you discover that there is another behind it. The next wave is just as nervously anxious and purposeful to swallow the lone figure up in its undertow. As each grey wall of water approached, it shut all else from the view of the determined woman who had escaped from the ghosts of the *Flying Dutchman*. It was not difficult to imagine that each particular wave was the final outburst of the ocean, the last effort of the determined water to claim her as she actually smiled at the white foamy tops of the waves which reminded Lynton of falling snow in her beloved Canada, and how she adored cuddling with Wayne by the fireplace as the soft flakes fell lightly on the ground outside their large picture window.

From the top of each wave, Lynton saw nothing but the vast expanse of the open sea. She felt that she was destined to die on that sea. Thoughts of her beloved Wayne flashed in her head. Then, she saw a faint light in the distance as the swirling wind slowly died away while the waves continued pushing and turning and washing all about her. Slowly the light seemed to move closer and closer. From a black line in the distance, the sea became bright in the spot where the light seemed to be. It was a ship. She knew it was a ship, and she looked down at the flashing beacon on her life tube. Surely, they would see her. Yes, they would see her.

Then, she saw the light in the distance move to her left, move away in a different direction. She thought, "If I am going to lose my life to the sea, why was I allowed to come this far and see a ship? Was I brought here merely to dragged away as I was about to taste the holy food of life?"

A night on the sea in a life tube is a long night indeed. As the shine of the light on the ship, lifting from the sea in the south, changed to full gold, it turned again in her direction. That light was the beacon of hope for a woman who longed to be in

          J. Wayne Frye

the arms of her beloved again, longed to feel safe and secure.

As the light kept coming, the white foamy crests of the waves rolled back and forth in the moonlight, and the soft wind brought the sound of the great sea's voice to her pounding heart. Suddenly, she did not feel so alone.

She could taste the saltiness of the sea when an occasional wave would pound into her face and she would swallow a bit of sea water. "Keep your mouth closed," she kept uttering to herself as she kept a stern eye on the light that was now moving more rapidly her way. She had seen lights out on the ocean when she was on the Wind Dancer, and grew to fear them, but this light was a light of life. It was bringing hope, not terror.

Occasionally, she was blinded by the water splashing in her eyes, and she was beginning to experience the agony of breathlessness. Then, blinking her salt laden eyes, she saw that the ship was really near now. At first, she could scarcely believe she saw a ship. Then, as she realized that indeed there was yet a chance of living, she became so enthusiastic that she started swimming toward the light.

Each stroke was not difficult at all, but was actually a life affirming melody of movement playing like a symphony of hope. She could hear the engines of the ship now, and they were pounding into her brain the realization that she was about to grasp life, real life with real people in the real world.

They pulled her from the sea and the captain, standing by the ladder rope that she was brought up on by two men, said, "Welcome aboard little lady."

Lynton & the Haunting
Of the HMS Wind Dancer

Epilogue
A Ship Filled with Ghosts

Leagues south, as fly the gull and hawk,
Cape Town watches with eyes that gawk;
Leagues south, the ocean roars with salt.
Lonely and wind-shorn, wood-forsaken,
With never a tree for spring to waken,
For tryst of lovers or farewells taken.
Circled by waters that never freeze,
Beaten by billow and swept by breeze,
The Dutchman and the Wind Dancer seize.
Set at the mouth of the Sound to hold
The coast lights up on its turret old,
Yellow with moss and sea-fog mould.

Dreary the land as wind gusts meet
At its doors and windows to howl and beat,
And ghosts take a token seat.
When Table Mountain is sweet with the brier-rose,
Hidden in the warm, soft dells are ghosts unclose,
And ships' ghosts in Cape Town someone knows.

Lynton & the Haunting
Of the HMS Wind Dancer

When boats to their morning fishing go,
And, held to the wind and slanting low,
Whitening and darkening the small sails show.
Then that lonely ocean seems so fair;
But the pale ghosts can be found there.
Oh, there is something evil in the air.

No greener valleys the sun invite,
On smoother beaches no sea-birds light,
No blue waves shatter to foam more white!
There, circling ever their narrow range,
Quaint tradition and legend strange
Live on unchallenged, and know no change.
And old men mending their nets of twine,
Talk together of dream and sign,
Of the Dutchman and Wind Dancer on line.
The ships that many years before,
Had ghosts for others in store,
As old men speak of the lore.

The eager Cape Towners one by one
Counted the shots of Dutchman's signal gun,
And watched Wind Dancer begin her run.
Into the teeth of death they sped,
And great mysteries they fed
Of sailors on deck long dead.
Oh men and brothers! What sights were there?
White upturned faces, hands stretched in prayer,
Where waves had pity, could ye not spare?
Down swooped the wreckers, like birds of prey
Tearing the heart of the ships away,
And the dead had never a word to say.

     J. Wayne Frye

Lynton & the Haunting
Of the HMS Wind Dancer

And then, with ghastly shimmer and shine
Over the rocks and the seething brine,
Dutchman and Wind Dancer were in line.
In cruelty as they onward sped,
The evil called them it is said,
And they are manned by the dead.
Nor looks, nor tones a doubt betray,
As is known to all, they quietly say:
"The ghosts will see another day."
Is there no death for a word once spoken?
Was never a deed but left its token
Written on tables never broken?

Both ships in malice's half,
Show shudder but never a laugh.
Phantom and shadow not in photograph.
For still, on many a moonless night,
From Table Mountain in moonlight
Spectres kindle and burn in sight.
Now low and dim, now clear and higher,
Leaps up the terrible Ghosts of Fire.
Will the flames of evil ever expire?
The wise skippers, though skies be fine,
Reef their sails when they see the sign
Of the Dutchman and the Wind Dancer in line.

Lynton, after drying off with a towel, stood in her still wet clothes, relating her harrowing experience to the captain of the Norwegian freighter and a few of the crew who stood spellbound. Wisely, she left out the part about the *Flying Dutchman* and the fantastic boarding of the

Wind Dancer by a ghost navy brandishing ancient sabres, for she knew no one would believe her.

Everyone there was enthralled with her harrowing tale, and was amazed at her valiant escape from the sinking ship. Their interest piqued, they hung on every word.

Finally, the captain, convinced the ship had gone down with all hands and passengers on board and having no way of locating her anyway, as no distress signal was ever received, realizing his negligence, asked her the name of the ship she had been on. She replied, "The Wind Dancer."

He looked at her with amazement, and said, "Lady, do you have a copy of your ticket?"

She remembered she had kept it in her pants pocket. She reached in and pulled out a wet and wrinkled ticket. She handed it to the captain, and he said, "Lady, look at the name of the ship on this ticket,"

She looked down at the ticket and the name seemed to pulsate out from the paper, and it slammed into her brain like a cold slap in the face. The name on the ticket was not Wind Dancer. It was *Wind Prancer*.

The captain said, "Lady, the Wind Dancer sunk in 1968. It went down with all hands and all passengers on board. No bodies were ever recovered, nor was the ship ever located."

Lynton knew then that she had simply boarded the wrong ship in Cape Town Harbour, a ship filled with ghosts!

The End

Lynton & the Haunting
Of the HMS Wind Dancer

The Real Lynton Viñas (The Dynamic Dynamo)

Every bit as daring and innovative as the fictional character, the real Lynton Viñas, having attended Cambridge School of Law and the International Hotcl School, is a marketing and hospitality management professional and author of *Haunted Hotels: Transitory Dances with the Dead*, *Grand Hotels: Reflections on Timeless Architectural Treasures*, *Astonishingly Remarkable and Unusual Hotels* and *A Concise Guide for Operating a Restaurant*.

DON'T MISS THE OTHER 13 BOOKS IN THE LYNTON SERIES BY J. WAYNE FRYE FROM FIRESIDE BOOKS.

Appendix – Flying Dutchman Legend

This ghost ship of the Cape of Good Hope near Cape Town, South Africa is the most famous of all sea phantoms. It has inspired poets, novelists and dramatists. Wagner even based an opera on the fearful tale.

Sir Walter Scott referred to a phantom ship in one of his poems, and his notes reveal that it was the Flying Dutchman he had in mind. He gave the impression that the legend was known to seamen in the first half of the seventeenth century. His version is an unusual one, for he speaks of a Flying Dutchman loaded with great wealth. Murder and piracy on board the ship were followed by an outbreak of plague among the crew. She sailed from port to port offering the ill-gotten wealth in return for shelter; but every harbour shut out the Flying Dutchman because of the plague. According to Scott the cause of her wandering was not altogether certain, and declared that the sighting of the doomed ship was considered by mariners to be the worst of all possible omens.

Far more familiar is the Van der Decken version, in which the Dutch captain is driving his ship mercilessly off the Cape of Good Hope in heavy weather. Sails are lost, decks are flooded, and the seamen beseech him to give up the attempt to round the Cape. Van der Decken lashes himself to the wheel and carries on, swearing that even God will not force him to change his mind. His

          J. Wayne Frye

blasphemous oath is heard. Out of the dark and ominous sky falls a brilliant shaft of light, and the Holy Ghost steps on to the deck. Van der Decken draws a pistol from his belt and fires. His arm falls withered at his side, and the Holy Ghost delivers sentence: "You have defied the wrath of God, and now you will sail these seas until the end of time. You will know thirst and hunger, but never will you know calm seas again. Henceforward you will bring misfortune to all who sight you."

Captain Owen, R.N., who charted long stretches of the South African Coast, declared that he saw the Flying Dutchman. The encounter appears in the logbook of H.M.S. Leven, dated 6 April 1823.

Owen was near Danger Point and bound for Simon's Bay, South Africa, when he thought he saw the H.M.S. Barracuda. This appearance surprised him as Barracuda had been ordered elsewhere. When he reached Simon's Bay he waited for a week before the Barracuda arrived. They compared log-books, and it was found that the two naval ships were three hundred miles apart when Owen intercepted the mystery ship.

Far more famous was the encounter near Danger Point witnessed by Prince Albert Victor and Prince George of Wales, later King George V. The young princes were both midshipmen, cruising in H.M.S. Bachante. The meeting was entered in the log-book as follows: "July 11, 1881. During the middle-watch the so called Flying Dutchman crossed our bows. She first appeared as a strange red light, as of a ship aglow, in the midst of which light her masts, spars and sails, seemingly those of a normal brig, some two hundred yards distant from us, stood out in long relief as she came up." Thirteen people altogether saw the ghost-ship. The sad fact was that the seaman who had first reported the phantom vessel fell from the fore-topmast crosstrees and was killed instantly. This was not the only death. The admiral in command of the squadron died at the next port of call.

London newspapers in 1911 published a message describing an American whaler off the Cape that had almost collided with a sailing ship believed to be the Flying Dutchman. Cape Town papers early in 1939 described a queer experience in False Bay, when people on the beaches saw a sailing ship heading up towards Muizenberg. It seemed that the ship would run into the breakers, but just before reaching the shallows she vanished. They all swore they had seen the Flying Dutchman.

The last recorded sighting was in 1942 off the coast of Cape Town. Four witnesses saw the Dutchman sail into Table Bay and disappear.

The author of this book lived in Cape Town for three years, as did the real Lynton Viñas, and we both heard many tales from old sailors about the Flying Dutchman. It is a tale that has lived on for hundreds of years, and like the Flying Dutchman itself, will, no doubt, live on until the end of time.

 J. Wayne Frye